# The Servants and the Beast

## Beast

In which the ones who saw it all tell the true tale of the Beast

Karen Blakely
R. A. Gates
Kelly Haworth
Jenniffer Lee
Cheryl Mahoney

ISBN-13: 978-1-68012-308-1

ISBN-10: 1-68012-308-4

First Edition

Cover Art by : Wynter Designs
https://www.facebook.com/groups/137242070277900/

# Table of Contents

# Chapter One:
## The Good Fairy

In which the Prince is very rude to the very wrong person

He really should not have been rude. Kind-hearted as I was, a Good Fairy dedicated to the highest principles of Goodness and Niceness, I normally tried to rise above that sort of thing. But some rudeness simply could not be borne–for the good of the rude person, naturally. And I always, always acted for the good of others. I was sure he'd thank me someday.

The whole little affair began on a snowy, blowy night. Just the sort of night for cozying up to a nice cup of tea, for petting an adorable pink kitten, or for wandering about in the snow disguised as an old crone, Testing Souls.

I pulled my carefully tattered gray cloak around me (so much goes into tattering a cloak just so, for that truly decrepit look—it's an art form) and shuffled up the long walk toward the main doors of the looming castle. I prided myself on my cronish shuffle. And I *never* went to a castle's backdoor. You didn't meet any princes that way, and I obviously had no time to waste on the souls of common folk. They just didn't have that royal quality.

I knocked on the castle doors, giving it a touch of magic to make the sound boom impressively through the building. That sort of thing ought to warn a person, but somehow it never did. While I waited for an answer, I checked to make sure my shimmering sparkles weren't spilling out of my cloak. They were piling up, but still hidden away for now.

At last the door swung open to a butler who, for a moment, looked quite regal and exceedingly proper in his brocaded waistcoat and elegant jacket. Then he saw me and frowned. "If you are looking for a hot meal, I can direct you to the kitchen entrance."

"Oh no, dearie, no!" I said, my voice high-pitched and quavering. For good measure, I added in my very best cackle. It was quite good. "I'm here to see your prince! I have a gift for him."

The butler's frown deepened. "Do you have an appointment?" he asked, in that tone of voice that indicated he was very sure I didn't.

"Yes, indeed," I said, nodding briskly. "Every lost soul has an appointment with their royal guardian on a cold night like this." This wasn't going to get me far with the butler, so I pushed past him. This, too, required just the right art. He made a grab for my cloak as I passed, but a subtle bit of magic whisked it out of his way.

"Now then," I said once I was inside. I shook snow off my cloak and looked over the two footmen standing in the hallway—both quite common fellows, one with long stringy hair and the other young, with freckles and big eyes. I did like how impressed common folk get. As they should.

I pointed a long bony finger at the freckled footman. "Where can I find your prince?"

He stammered for a moment, then blurted, "...in the ballroom?"

"Oh, is there a party? I do *love* parties!" I exclaimed, clasping my hands together. I didn't need directions to the ballroom. I had been to this castle before, if a few generations previous. I set off, ignoring the futile protests of the butler behind me.

I turned a corner, and nearly collided with a weeping woman standing in the hallway with a big armful of books. What a perfectly ridiculous place to stand weeping. I attempted to continue my cronish shuffle past without paying her any further attention.

She blinked, staring at me. "Who…?" she began.

"Business with the Prince, dearie!" I said with another cackle.

"He's not in a good mood," she murmured.

Well, perhaps he wasn't in a good mood for weeping women. I *never* indulged in such nonsense. I walked on, letting no other servants I passed deter me from my mission. Most ignored me as I ignored them. I turned another corner and went past the library, glancing through the door just long enough to see a man balanced at the top of a sliding ladder, straightening a portrait, while a dark-haired young woman steadied the ladder below. How nice to see servants performing a useful function. A good sign.

It was not so good a sign when I encountered another footman, this one quite stocky, deep in the castle and bolder than the two by the front door. He dared to step forward and reach for my arm. "Aren't you lost?"

"Business with the Prince," I said again, more firmly, and waved him off, putting magic behind the gesture. He stumbled backwards and clumsily crashed into a suit of armor, sending it falling to pieces in a very unpleasant clatter. I sniffed my disapproval and skirted around him.

I could hear music playing somewhere through the halls, likely a piano, but it didn't seem to be from the direction of the ballroom. I couldn't imagine why someone would be playing a piano in a room away from a party. Another poor sign about the state of affairs in this castle.

And sure enough, when I arrived in the ballroom I saw no signs of a party. The Prince was in there, surrounded by any number of swords and axes and things, swinging away at ugly padded practice dummies. It was all so uncouth and did not bode well.

"Helloooo, dearie!" I called as I descended the sweeping stairs. "I've come with a gift for you."

The Prince stopped waving his sword and leaned on it instead, its point digging crudely into the polished wooden floor. He stared at me with a contemptuous curl of his lip. "Who the devil are you? How did you get in?"

"Oh, I go where I like," I said. "Now, if you offer me food and shelter and ask *nicely*, I'll give you a wonderful reward." My rewards really were wonderful. I prided myself on them too. I gave enchanted cloaks, magical palaces, dresses that shine like the sun, talking goats…all the things that a truly proper prince or princess needed.

The Prince wiped his sweaty forehead with the back of one arm, pushing back a flop of matted dark hair. It was cold outside but flames were roaring in the large fireplace along one wall, and he had evidently been flailing about with weapons for some time. "I have no time to waste on ridiculous old hags. Now go away and stop bothering me."

I also prided myself on my curses, for severity and importance of the moral lessons involved. And this was not going well. I shook my finger at him. "You are not being polite. If you apologize at once, I *may* forgive you. But you have already forfeited the chance at one of my very *nicest* gifts."

"I told you to go away," he growled, face contorting into a glare. "You won't like it if I have to say it again." He picked up an ax, and turned back to his padded dummy.

"I'm *warning* you," I said, because let no one say that I was not *very* fair and generous.

"And *I* warned you—now get out of here, you ugly old woman!" the Prince thundered, and this time when he hoisted the ax higher, he didn't seem to be aiming it towards the dummy.

I shook my head in sorrow. I was always so sad to see someone be this foolish. "That was not the correct response."

And then I flung my arms out, cloak bursting open in a great spray of pent-up gold and pink sparkles. In the center of the cloud I transformed into my true self, wearing my best pink dress and my favorite pink wings.

The Prince stumbled backward, eyes widening. "Wha— what are you?"

"I," I said grandly, "am a Good Fairy."

His eyes got even bigger, face twisting into horror. Or maybe respectful awe. Yes, that was much more likely. "Oh no."

It was a good sign to see such immediate remorse for his rudeness, and I thought there might be hope for him after all. With the right corrective action. "You have shown me your true self," I said severely, "and you did not prove worthy of my gifts. Instead—"

He fell to his knees, face white. "No, no, I'm sorry! I didn't realize—I didn't mean—"

"It is too late," I said with a wave of one hand, sending another artful spray of sparkles across the room. "But do not worry. I am a *Good* Fairy, and I am dedicated to serving others. I'm going to *help* you!"

"Please," he said in strangled tones, "please, don't."

I disregarded this. He was unworthy of my gifts, but not of my lessons. Besides, gold sparkles were already shooting out of my hands, swirling around the kneeling Prince. He covered his face as the storm of sparkles knocked him backwards to sprawl on the floor. In seconds, fur was sprouting between his fingers—and everywhere else too, while his body grew to an impressive seven feet with proportioned shoulders and a very nice tail.

"What are you *doing* to me?" he shouted, as magnificent horns sprouted from his forehead.

The horns were the last step. I surveyed him critically. Big, furry, a bit scary but not *entirely* vicious in appearance. Perfect. "I turned you into a Beast," I explained.

"Change me back!" he roared, voice deepened to a suitable pitch for a Beast, as he staggered to his feet and took a step toward me.

"Quite impossible," I said, rising up into the air. I wouldn't want him to make matters worse by doing something drastic. "A Beast you are, and a Beast you will remain, until you learn to see past appearances and find True Love. You may thank me now."

He stared at me for a few seconds, then with an inarticulate growl he took a swipe at me with his new claws.

Of course he missed, but I rose a bit farther anyway, a drift of gold and pink sparkles below my feet. "Or you may thank me later," I amended. People were *so* slow to understand how I benefited them. He'd work it out eventually. "I believe my work here is done for now."

Then I paused, cocked my head slightly, and said, "But of course, no one becomes a nasty brute all by himself. People haven't taught you very well, have they?"

"If I catch you, you hideous, horrible—"

"Yes, yes," I said soothingly, waggled my fingers, and sent a wave of magic rocking through the castle. This whole beastly affair might well go on for decades, and it wouldn't do for all the servants to get old and die in the meantime. Much better to transform them into shapes that would still be useful, but keep them going as needed. And no doubt they'd learn something too. I do love it when I can spread good lessons to an entire castle.

I floated out of the ballroom where the Prince was continuing to bellow, and flew toward the front hall. I could feel my spell spreading as I went, and I smiled as I watched it take effect.

There was that rude footman who had tried to stop me earlier—he was attempting to reassemble the suit of armor he'd so awkwardly knocked over. When my magic reached him he gave a shudder, and a pink glow surrounded him as he thinned, grew transparent, and dissolved into the armor. A moment later the armor shook its helmet and took an uncertain step forward.

The library—the man in the painting was now leaning out, demanding explanations, while the ladder below him rocked in confused agitation.

And here was that weeping woman, looking around her in alarm as she heard outcries and exclamations around the castle. She stared at me as I approached, backing up and bumping into a low bookcase set against the wall.

"What is happening?" she asked in frightened tones.

"No need to be upset," I said soothingly. "It's just a curse. And it will all be so much better for everyone in the end!"

I couldn't tell if she was paying attention to my words, as a pink glow overtook her at that moment. An instant more and she had been absorbed into the bookcase, her dropped books slotting neatly into place on the shelves. How very tidy.

I could feel that my magic had reached nearly all the castle by now, just as I neared the front doors. I was in time to see the stringy-haired footman, busily mopping up puddles in the hallway, merge with his mop, while the butler was swallowed up by one of the armchairs lining the hall.

The freckled footman who had been so impressed by me gave a startled cry and dived behind the coat rack. As though that would stop my magic, silly man. But perhaps he'd like being a coat rack. It was certainly more durable than being a fragile human.

I shook off a few sparkles, which sprinkled over the floor of the hall and gave it a much brighter aspect. The sparkles would multiply in my absence, reminding everyone of the gravity of the situation they had regrettably gotten themselves into. Then I gave a cheery wave to the coat rack, armchair and mop, opened the front doors with another gesture of my hand, and flew off into the stormy night.

*Such* a productive evening. I felt very good about this.

# Chapter Two:
## Meanwhile, Elsewhere in the Castle...

In which the plans of the pianist, the artist, and the scribe are
buried by dust

**M**aneuvering through the large and desolate
castle, I heard a resounding knock at the front
door. I took pause long enough to hear an old
woman cackle a need to see the Prince himself. Perhaps I
could have waited, but I left Theodore to handle that proper
mess and moved on. There was simply no time left to waste.

Composing symphonies was my life; it breathed through
me with great purpose. But, even with my expertise, the
Prince had twisted my teaching over the last decade to that
of his own desires, which only pushed me to find work
elsewhere. Now, everything was ready for my departure, and
I could never leave my beloved Rebecca behind.

Stopping in front of the golden mirror in the hall, I
straightened my chestnut hair and shifted my blue coat and
white ascot. Finally, I checked the quality of my straight
toothed smile; all was in order for a night of proper wooing.
After years of quiet flirting, I knew Rebecca fancied me, but
did she love me? The wind howled outside the stone walls
and I hesitated--it was snowing and freezing, not exactly the
best time to leave a warm castle. But I had made all the
proper arrangements and by morning I would be a new man
with the woman who would run away with me. Well, if she
agreed.

I found Darwin, the castle guard and my only confidant, near the entrance on the way to the study. He nodded as he left his post and followed me until I found her. Darwin knew of my love for Rebecca, and had thus promised to keep watch outside the doorway, until the Prince required him otherwise.

Rebecca sat in the late Queen's study watching the evening snowfall. The frayed snow dropped through the gilded light beyond the petulant clouds, and she watched it with the eyes of a master.

She had an easel with her, an old one that she said creaked with inspiration, and her paints were organized neatly on a table beside her. Instead of canvas, Rebecca used a flat board with wrinkled parchment attached for her current project, which was outlined lightly in pencil.

Rebecca's right hand cradled a thick wooden brush and she stretched, which allowed her long chestnut braid to slip over her shoulder and alongside of her left breast. Her gown was simple and elegant, a shade of pale blue against the soft bronze of her skin.

Rebecca leaned over and began her paint selection as I approached. "My lady, begging your pardon. But, might I show you something?"

She turned and smiled as her eyes, dark and rich, met my own. She set down her brush and said, "What a nice surprise, Monsieur Stein!"

The joy on her face fed the longing in my heart. I bowed at the waist. "Maximus, please." Rising, I brought the canvas from behind my back. "Would you perhaps paint on this?"

Her eyes widened as she saw the treasure in my hands, "Oh, that canvas is lovely!"

"Do you like it?" I could provide these for her now with my new employment, but would it be enough?

Her mouth formed an adorable circle before she covered it lightly with her skilled hands. "This is wonderful, Monsieur."

I leaned forward and placed the canvas gingerly in front of the parchment on her easel—the air was immediately sweeter with the scent of her perfume, a rose blend. I took her hand in mine and without thinking I raised her hand to my lips and kissed her smooth skin before looking her in the eyes. "My lady, you must know by now my love for you."

Rebecca's warm eyes darted toward the entrance of the study as I continued, "He is training in the ballroom at the present." I smirked a bit as the cloaked woman crossed my mind. "I'm fairly certain Theodore might have a distraction for the Prince to buy us a little more time. We are entirely private."

She relaxed but removed her hand all the same. "Monsieur—"

"Maximus."

Her skin flushed along the curve of her cheek and she laughed before saying, "Maximus. I am aware of my own feelings, and of the rules that are set upon us. His Highness would never allow us to be together."

"I have enough wages to set us up, and an offer to work for the Duke of Versailles." I released her hands and bowed grandly. "He is very interested in the great Maximus Stein." I lowered to a kneel in front of Rebecca, my heart in my hands. "My love, my profession sings with music, but my heart beats for you. I leave tonight, but I couldn't possibly leave without you. Will you come with me and journey into a new life together?"

She opened her mouth to respond, and my gut wanted to say she was going to accept my proposal, but we were cruelly interrupted. Darwin announced in his deep boom of a voice, "Monsieur Quillsby, what is your service in the study tonight?"

Quillsby, his animated gestures only partially blocked by Darwin's large arm, flared wildly with a flurry of words as he tried to bustle into the room. "My purpose? It is Sunday is it not? I am required to be here for whatever class the Prince so chooses to be mentored in for the evening."

Darwin, ever the friend, peeked around the corner and blocked the entryway to give me time to rise. Rebecca's eyes stayed with my own as I, acting as if I were simply buckling my shoes before sitting at the grand, although withering, piano; I had managed to keep the piano in perfect pitch and I had pride in that.

As I thought of the lesson the Prince might pay attention to, I heard his highness shouting from down the halls. It began as shouts and somehow morphed into a guttural growl that echoed across the barren castle, lingering and growing with reverberation. A cackle I didn't recognize drowned in replacing menace as just noise.

Curiosity peaked and then pushed aside as my focus returned to Rebecca. I kept eye contact and said firmly, "Please consider my offer." Rebecca bit her bottom lip, released, and resumed her position at the easel.

Quillsby continued to argue with Darwin, growing more and more ruffled, to say the least. "My word! Do move aside, Monsieur LeGrand!" He bustled into the room adjusting his black coat then straightening the supplies he carried in with him. "Thank you. Well, I say." His eyes focused on Rebecca and me, and he asserted with more chatter. "I have had it now! I am finished! That boy prince! Well, our fair Queen Marie never would approve. He's in the ballroom this very moment, fighting with a wretchedly dressed woman. Poor soul probably just needs a hot meal and he won't give her the time of day!" He shook his head pointedly.

Quillsby dipped the tip of his favorite quill in the tiny ink pot he'd carried in with him. He began writing along the once used parchment, but after a few strokes he scoffed, "Absurd! How am I to teach if I have no proper materials! Used parchment! Dry inkwells?" He acted as if he would throw the very quill in his hand but thought better of it and gently placed it within an inside pocket of his coat. He sneezed, a claim that he was prone to sneezing fits due to the regular dust of inactivity of the castle, and the flecks flitted about his face. He glanced at his pocket watch that he kept in his vest. "These horrible allergies just get worse for me." He removed a well-used hanky and sneezed audibly into it before saying, "Well, of course the Prince is late. I wonder if he'll even show up tonight. Whose turn is it, anyway?"

I organized sheet music on the piano. "You know he won't decide who will bear the weight of teaching until he arrives."

Quillsby sniffed, "Well, the dear late Queen was never so irresponsible with our precious time."

Rebecca's voice rippled with layers that resembled thick brush strokes; raspy and warm. "Monsieur Quillsby, I agree. Queen Marie was quite lovely. Most days."

Quillsby acted physically damaged and slumped down. "What could you possibly mean by that?"

Rebecca turned and gestured to a large painting above the fireplace on the opposite wall. "Her complexity ran deep, pulling her away for long periods of time." She rested her chin on her hand. "I hoped art might help her find the peace she sought."

Quillsby shook his head decisively, his thick unruly hair wriggling about his brow. "Well, a woman of her lovely stature could never find peace knowing what her son has done—"

She held up a gentle hand, "Of course, you're right, dear Monsieur Quillsby. I tremble with fear when he approaches my works for I never know if he will destroy my pieces or spare them. But, the fair Queen would still love him."

The writer sighed, dust poofing out in a large circle from the sheer energy of the air he produced. "Well, I am most certainly NOT the late Queen."

At this point I offered a loud yawn, reveling in how it sounded pitch perfect from a tuning fork. I stretched my long fingers in a momentary pause.

The Prince was cruel in the way he handled his affairs with merchants by short-changing them for hard work, and his anger pushed some of his staff to a point of fear; I never thought of the Prince as anything more than a boy. He had much to learn and not an ear to hear of it.

I played the beginning of a tune that I knew was Rebecca's favorite. She watched me as I played. Above the music I said, "Quillsby, of course you aren't anything like the fair Queen! She was the heart of this castle, not the blow hard."

"Well, I never—"

The keys danced elegantly. "Relax, old friend." I sighed and lowered the intensity of the song play with a higher pitched, fairy melody, while Rebecca adjusted her hair and smiled toward her lap. She met my gaze and I winked.

Quillsby dusted the shoulder pad of his black workman's coat. "Monsieur Stein, it is appalling how you tease the ladies."

He never did care for my flirtation with Rebecca, which made me enjoy it all the more; I laughed heartily, a deep lingering sound in my chest before saying, "Ah, Quillsby. No one asked you. Besides, you're so up in arms against the Prince, rightly so of course, but you can't entirely blame the boy. His father was cruel and his fair mother died when he was so young. How else could he have learned her joy if he's forgotten it?"

"Are you making excuses for that ingrate?"

I paused the music and looked at Quillsby. "Of course not. His choices are his own. I'm merely stating that he comes by it more honestly than not." I maintained focus on Quillsby until the writer nodded and acknowledged we were indeed soldiers of a familiar truth.

There was a sound in the distant hall, animal-like and enraged. It was unlike anything I had ever heard before. We paused in our conversation before Rebecca rose from her stool and sat down next to me on the once well-padded bench, placing her hands over mine on the keys. She glanced toward the doorway and said, "Did you hear that? You don't think an animal found passage inside, do you?"

I shook my head, "No, of course not. His Majesty is probably annoyed with the old woman."

Rebecca smiled. Her presence stole away my interest in what happened in the ballroom, and I began to play again, but a simple tune so that she could keep her hands on mine. The softness of her fingers crept into the longing I felt for her.

She had yet to accept my proposal. I looked into her eyes as we sat together, hoping she would say something but just as she opened her mouth the calm of the room shifted into a dissonant rage that flowed freely from down the hall.

Pink dust and resounding rage littered over our bodies; a feeling of discontent and disaster all in one sensation. There was an eerie glow that permeated through the open doorway, pink and obnoxious. The roaring down the hall pulled a shiver along the edge of my spine. The feel of the space strengthened my motive to leave, and soon, but I could not just force Rebecca to do something she did not care to.

Rebecca's sincere eyes found my own. I stopped playing and lifted her right hand to my lips; I whispered against the smoothness of her perfect skin, "Do you have an answer my love?"

Her breath rose and fell with a gentle rapidness and when she spoke every fiber of my body held onto her words. If she agreed, then the Prince would no longer have a hold on us and we could be free to live a life together. She gestured toward the kitchen where I knew her favorite friends worked, the castle chef and wash maids. "Well, Maximus. I can't leave without a proper goodbye, now can I?" She reached to my hair and ran her fingers over the sides as she whispered, "My love—"

Quillsby, who clearly had enough of being a third wheel, sauntered over and bowed ever dramatically. "Not that the two of you care! But, it would seem we are not working tonight. So, good day and until next time."

Rebecca pulled back, patted my cheek warmly. "Meet me in here after the Prince retires for the evening. We can talk then." She turned to Quillsby. " Monsieur Quillsby, would you be so kind as to escort me back to my room?"

He held out the crook of his elbow in response, and while I couldn't see his face, I detected a hint of a smile behind the frowning contour of his chin. I watched them from the lid of the piano as Rebecca collected her canvas from her easel. Rebecca looked over her shoulder at me, and a smile crept across my face. Because there was a very good reason why she never asked me to walk her to her room.

As they stood to leave, they stalled at the sound of our prince's outrage. The discontent I felt moments before lurched then with color blasts and restraints. Suddenly, I knew. The cackle, the pink dust—this was the workings of an evil fairy!

The magic at hand somehow exhaled heavily through the glittery air and wrenched my body, painfully shifting my quick moving limbs into tedious slow motion. I reached for Rebecca, at least, I tried. But my arms became heavy and solid like wooden planks wrought together. My face and eyes and legs changed and swerved my balance. I feared sickness as I trembled over the floorboards. When I spoke my words were deep keys from the piano I adored so much, my hands were no longer hands, and my voice no longer my own.

Even without my seemingly natural eyes, I still managed to see the fear morph over Rebecca's body she shouted my name across the room before she was absorbed into the very easel she touched, her beauty and demeanor lost on the blank canvas I had brought for her. I tried to call out, but the piano keys were all that effort produced.

I didn't see Quillsby at first, but I guessed by the flighty, fidgeting feather that bounced from one spot of the room to the next that he too had transformed, and into the quill he kept so diligently in his front pocket. We were all trapped and lost souls now.

Five years later, the study that held me captive gave me a perfect view of the sunset over the western mountains. Tonight, the oranges and yellows bled through the dark grey and blue that pulled past the evening light. The stars brightened the darkness in the distance. While I used to play with my dreams over those stars, each passing year imprisoned as a piano stole more of what had made me a masterful musician. The stars that once were glorious and whimsical for song inspiration were now foreboding and as out of reach as the dreams they once represented.

Of course, I reminded myself that there were worse things than being bound to the glory of a grand piano sitting in a spacious study situated with large windows. After all, I could be stuck in the dusty library as a portrait, or as a dishrag in the kitchen, or heaven forbid I be confined as a footstool.

My slatted eyes, which I presumed were no longer the green irises I was born with, but instead some strange facet along the piano edge, lingered on the wooden easel nestled on the right side of the closest window to the grand marble fireplace. My ivory keys trembled deeply before I silenced them with a jerk. Rebecca had found her way back to the window, again. Forever the artist trapped in the wooden frame that once held her creations.

My strings tightened as I watched her against the tattered, red silk curtains. The pink sparkles that seemed to spawn from our curse lingered lightly along her edges as she viewed the sky in silence, her easel angling just slightly to the right and maneuvering left as she analyzed the scene. How my heart ached in the soundboard of my center. It beat no more yet still it pined for her because I could still see her beyond the easel she had been forced to become.

Quillsby fluttered into the room, very much like he fluttered as a man, saying, "Ah, splendid. I thought I would find you in here, Mademoiselle." He wriggled as he floated and settled in upon the fireplace mantel. "And hello, Stein. Are you even awake this time?"

I slammed all my keys in heavy fashion, startling the quill so much he fell to the glitter dusted floor sputtering, "Well, I say! Stein, how awful you are to—"

Rebecca creaked as she turned to face us, her canvas blank and her voice raspy. "Now, now, gentlemen. Maximus, that was a bit unkind."

I spoke, the vibrations of my soundboard muffling my usual tenor with a mix of layered piano tones: "Of course, I know you're right. But it was a great bit of fun that I don't have much opportunity for these days." I turned carefully on the wheels that I was grateful to have, "Monsieur Quillsby, I do apologize. I simply could not resist."

Quillsby had puffed up but now relaxed into a more slender profile, "I forgive you but only because I am more noble than you." He fluttered over to Rebecca and rested gingerly along the top of her canvas. Jealousy stung through me, even as a piano.

I bit my sound down and muttered in a low growl, "What is it, that you need to grace us with your presence, Quillsby?"

He relaxed comfortably along the length of the canvas that Rebecca kept blank for the time being, and said, "It has been five years to this day that we were transformed."

I rolled back to the dented floorboards that I had come to know as my resting ground. "This is not news."

Quillsby hesitated and then said, "I know. But, it felt fitting to return and be with the scholars I once collaborated with."

Rebecca's voice, softer than the bite of my own voice, came through and said, "We are honored, Quillsby." She turned her canvas toward me and said, "Memories are all that we have."

I began the key movement involved with Rebecca's favorite song as the sun dipped deeper behind the mountainside, the reds oozing beyond the white of the mountain peaks. I sighed, "Another day lost." The words rang more than I meant for them to.

Rebecca heard me. "But hope still dances on the backside of the stars."

I didn't reply and instead played out the song of my heart for her, waiting for the day that her sweet hope would come to fruition. Although, with the Prince's fall into beastly nonsense in both body and spirit, I doubted her hopes would blossom into reality.

# Chapter Three:
## A Young Lady Arrives

In which a visitor interrupts the reading of the castle
librarian

We lost track of time very quickly, my friend Isadora and I. It's hard to keep a proper account of days when you're a sliding ladder and a figure trapped in a painting, respectively. We did well tracking hours, since the tall windows in the castle's multistory library let in an expansive amount of light, be it of sun or moon. But days all blurred together in this strange new life. Before, I had been the castle librarian, Hugo Livre, and Isadora had served as my assistant. Now, we were fellow victims in this strange curse, unsure if we would ever escape.

At least until the day the first changes came. Our first hope. That day, I believe several years into the curse, began normally enough. As much as you could talk about normalcy under the circumstances. I woke up curled in the large armchair I was painted into—sometimes I regretted the lack of a bed in the picture—and called a cheery good morning to Isadora.

"Good morning, Hugo," she called back, sliding toward me from her venturing around the perimeter of the circular library. The carved figure on the ladder that enabled Isadora to see and speak was fortunately at the same level as my painting, both of us some twelve feet off the ground. She could have been another twenty feet above me, up near the ceiling, making conversation horribly difficult.

In past days, I had always insisted on formality, and she had called me a very proper Monsieur Livre. But in our new trials, we had found it better to be friendlier. All around the castle, servants who had formerly gone by their family names were increasingly known by their first names, and I accepted that this was a matter of decorum that might be better relaxed.

I stretched, getting the kinks out of my painted shoulders, and leaned on the edge of my frame, automatically brushing away the light coating of pink and gold sparkles that invariably appeared overnight. I could see that dust was accumulating on the books as well, but as I couldn't reach them I tried my best to put it out of my mind.

I could not, alas, climb out of my painting. I had tried that, the first terrible day when we found ourselves so strangely altered. Any attempts to leap out of the square that bounded my world bounced me right back in and jarred me not a little. And I did wonder what kind of state I'd be in if I could leap out, seeing as my feet weren't painted in.

"What should we read today?" I asked, because at least I could lean and reach out. My painting hung right in with the bookshelves (north wall, amongst shelves 12 through 17). The way books lined every part of the room, it would have been impossible for me to be placed anywhere else. As it was, being a large painting I could reach a dozen shelves around me, and the volumes upon them.

"Perhaps…some history for a change?" Isadora said in teasing tones, a little of the squeak of her ladder coming out in her voice.

I was in the history section. History was *all* I could reach. I had not always approved of Isadora's sense of humor when we were human—libraries are quiet, serious places, and the ordering of books should not be treated with levity or irreverence—but now I found her light-hearted nature a comfort.

Although Isadora had free range of movement, she could no longer lift even a pamphlet off a shelf, locked as she was into a ladder with no arms. I regretted the lack of access to the botanical guides (west wall, shelves five, six, and part of seven), but at least I wasn't in amongst the fairy tales (south wall, shelves three through eight). Silly things, fairy tales. So unrealistic.

I reached down to the shelf just below me. "Perhaps local history? We read global yesterday."

"Just so long as it isn't recent history," Isadora said with a slight sniff. "I am *not* interested in hearing about his royal beastliness."

Isadora was a kind-hearted soul, but she harbored resentment toward a certain royal personage. I couldn't say I disagreed.

"I *still* don't see why we got cursed because *he* was rude," Isadora muttered, rocking back and forth along the shelves in her irritation. "Didn't we always try to direct him toward the nicest reading choices? It's not *our* fault he wanted to study warfare and princely privileges, instead of your charming botanical guides."

"It is hard to see how anyone with a proper appreciation for the beauties of plants could grow up arrogant and discourteous," I agreed, rifling through the pages of the book I had selected. "This has a chapter on His Highness' parents, but most is earlier ancestry."

"Good enough," Isadora said, and while I can't exactly explain how a sliding ladder can settle comfortably into place, she somehow did. "I always enjoy your reading, you know."

"A proper reading voice is of course a requirement of my position," I remarked, though it was not unpleasant to hear the commendation. I reclined in my chair and plucked an apple from the bowl of fruit painted beside me. A new one always reappeared a moment after I seized one. I didn't need to eat, but the habit did make things more pleasantly homey. Pity I wasn't painted with a bottle of wine—but at least it was a variety fruit basket, each item painted at the peak of freshness. Unripe apples would have palled quickly.

"Chapter One," I began. I happened to glance out toward the window across the way. And stopped reading.

"Hugo?" Isadora prompted after a moment. "Is something wrong with the book?"

My voice emerged in a strangled croak that was quite unintelligible. I coughed, tried again. "A woman. There's a *woman* on the front lawn!"

"Really?" Isadora said in a high-pitched squeak, as she whizzed over to the window. It was a sign of her excitement that she bothered, because we had learned long ago that her eyes were pointed the wrong way to look out when positioned in front of the window. "Ergh," she said inarticulately, and whizzed back around the circle to find an angle she could see from.

The woman seemed to be a tall, willowy creature, with vivid red hair and an equally vivid purple dress that I suspected were not meant to be matched (fashion, east wall, shelf 10). I couldn't see a great deal from this distance, but she did seem to be looking up toward the castle and striding forward with purposeful interest.

"Do you think she can break the curse?" I asked, gripping the edge of my frame in my anxiety. "Didn't that mad fairy say that if His Highness fell in love—?"

"Yes, yes!" Isadora said eagerly. "I hope they like each other! And that he behaves!"

I was already leaping to new plans and ideas. "So they meet, he probably won't make a sterling first impression but give it a little time…what do you think, freed from the curse in a couple of weeks?"

"Some men take much longer to fall in love than that," Isadora said, suddenly sounding offended. "Or at least to realize it."

I couldn't see what I had said to upset her—I usually was very good at keeping to social etiquette (east wall, shelves one through nine). "What's wrong?" I asked.

"Nothing," she said in shorter tones than usual, and somehow managed to give the impression of flouncing off as she whizzed away again.

Women. Hopefully this new arrival would be calmer. She had already disappeared from view, heading for the front door. I leaned back in my armchair, peeled an orange, and thought about how wonderful it was going to be to get out of this painting. I could hardly remember the last time I'd seen a plant up close.

An hour or so later we heard the Prince roaring in the distance. He grew inarticulate in moments of rage, but presumably it was something to do with the woman. I exchanged an uneasy glance with Isadora, who had given up being offended. "Well, we didn't expect a positive start," I pointed out. But surely the Prince knew how important this was. Surely once he calmed down, he'd try to be agreeable?

After the roaring had faded away, Isadora circled around as close as she could to the door. "Lady Jayne!" she called. "Did you see what happened?"

Once Queen Marie's secretary, Lady Jayne was now a bookcase, trapped in the front hall. She could see more of what went on than Isadora and I—but we had more books in our reach. The front hall was a long way to call to, but it was just possible when the situation seemed urgent enough.

"Oh, my dear, it was simply terrible!" Lady Jayne called back, voice refined even as she projected across the distance between us. "A young woman has arrived, and His Highness was perfectly awful to her! She went into his study and was looking in his desk when His Highness found her. He…took it badly."

I knew Lady Jayne of old and she was always discreet. His Highness must have taken it very badly indeed.

"But what happened?" Isadora called. "What did he do?"

A pause, then her words came in a rush, as though she couldn't help herself. "He ranted and roared and hauled that poor girl off to the North Tower!"

I moaned. "What is he thinking? He can't woo a woman by throwing her in the tower! She must hate him."

"That's better than not being noticed," Isadora remarked, rather obscurely I felt, since you could hardly not notice His Highness, pre- or post-curse.

"Perhaps he'll calm down and apologize," Lady Jayne suggested, but did not sound hopeful at all.

Nor did it seem a hopeful sign when we heard distant bellowing shortly later. Distant, but growing closer. The Prince was returning from the North Tower, and he had not calmed down.

As loud as he was, I soon was able to distinguish his words. "Stupid, mocking woman! She was staring at me, I know she was. Like I'm some kind of freak! Because I *am* a freak! I used to be so handsome, any woman might have loved me then, but *now*—now that horrible fairy has turned me into this *monster*. I know that's all she'll ever see me as…" The words trailed away into a deep, inarticulate growl that was even more alarming. Especially because by now he was in the hallway outside the library.

I shrank down in my armchair, desperately hoping that he wouldn't turn in at our door. It still gave me shudders to remember the most recent time he'd entered this room. We often heard roaring from elsewhere in the castle, but His Highness came into the library only occasionally. And that was more than often enough.

Last time he'd come tearing in shouting about that evil fairy who cursed him and knocked every fairy tale off of the shelves. They'd crashed to the ground in a flurry of pages and little puffs of sparkles. Even those silly stories didn't deserve *that*. My painted heart had ached to see the piles of tumbled books strewn across the floor. The Beast had shoved over two armchairs and thundered out again, without so much as acknowledging Isadora and myself.

I had been too depressed even to read, despite all Isadora's efforts to cheer me. Finally Darwin, a castle guard turned into a suit of armor, had wandered in. At our urging and with our directions, he put the fallen books back into place, giving me renewed courage to carry on.

His Highness had been known to throw a book or two before the curse came upon us, but it had only grown worse since he was enchanted.

The rumbling growl of the Prince's voice grew ever closer now, though I could catch only an occasional articulate word. Something like "monster" and "mocking" and "all laughing." Even worse, the sound of his voice was accompanied by a scratching, scraping noise. Other servants, able to move around, had told us that His Highness had taken to running his claws along the walls, leaving long furrowed scratches in his wake.

I held my breath as he came closer, closer…and passed on beyond our doorway.

I relaxed again in my chair, though my relief was short-lived. My lovely books might be safe for the moment, but there was still the larger situation to think of. With Lady Jayne despondent, Isadora baffling, and the Prince making very poor choices regarding this visiting woman, I was sorely pressed to remain positive.

It did not help that we could do nothing now but wait for further developments. The suspense was dreadful. I had never even liked mystery novels (south wall, shelves 38 through 42).

The next morning, activity finally began again. It was so frustrating to be trapped in the library, where we could hear distant footsteps and voices, but couldn't learn what was happening. I paced within the narrow confines of my painting—well, as much as I could without feet—and kept my gaze on the open doorway, hoping for someone with news.

First, I thought I heard voices away down the hall somewhere—possibly the Prince, possibly the higher-pitched notes of a woman's voice. Had he repented of his temper, let her out of the tower, and begun a more proper wooing? Perhaps all was not lost yet!

While the voices were still distant, a thudding sound approached. I had learned to interpret many sounds as people on the move, now that so many of us lacked feet in one way or another, and was not surprised when two figures appeared passing our doorway.

They were two of the castle musicians, now transformed like the rest of us, in the imposing form of Charles, a fine cello, and the much smaller shape of Victor, a violin. I used to direct them to the music section of the library (east wall, shelves 16 through 29), and we had had many gratifying discussions on musical history and form.

"Charles, Victor, what is going on?" I asked.

"No time!" Charles snapped, barely even pausing in the doorway. "We have to hide!"

"But why?" I asked, baffled by this unfriendly and unhelpful behavior. I had never seen Charles try to avoid the fairer sex before either, so this was doubly confusing.

The only response was a few mournful notes from Victor, and then they had disappeared beyond the doorway.

"They seemed almost frightened," Isadora said with concern in her voice. "What do you suppose they're hiding from? His Highness?"

Before I could formulate a response, a second figure appeared in the doorway, and this one fortunately entered.

In fact, Archambault came careening into the library and slammed the door behind him, leaning back against it and panting. Once a footman, he was now a coat rack, his speckled wood enlivened by a pink fur coat (definitely not its natural color: animal biology, west wall, shelves 18 through 21) hanging from one branch, and an enormous feathered hat on top. They didn't seem the usual sort of clothes for a young footman, but he held onto them, for reasons I had never inquired about. Today he seemed to have added an extra white feather to his hat.

"Hello, Archambault!" Isadora said, sliding around toward him. "What can you tell us about the girl?"

"His Highness let her out of the tower today. And she's…loud," Archambault said after a moment. "Very loud. And…interested in things."

He had a horrified expression on his speckled wood, which alarmed me but didn't stop Isadora from saying, "Well? Go on, tell us more of what happened!"

"It's good the Prince let her out of the tower, right?" I prompted.

At that moment the extra feather detached itself from Archambault's hat, and I recognized the transformed shape of Quillsby, castle scribe. He floated over to the nearest bookshelf and perched on the edge, fluffing himself importantly. "One can only hope this is a positive progression of events, but I am none too sure," he announced. "He did let her out, but he was not at all gracious about the matter."

"He told her she was irritating," Archambault said faintly. "She stood at the door to the cell and complained. Loudly. About how this was not appropriate behavior and she deserved better and all that."

"Yes, yes, quite," Quillsby said, whisking himself up to a higher shelf. "And now they are exploring the castle together, which may fall under the broadest definition of courting, but I do not feel he is exerting himself as he might. I think he ought to try a little bit harder, and I was about to inform him so when this footman ran off with me tangled in his hat!"

Archambault shuddered, pink coat swaying. "She was commenting. Loudly. On *everything*."

"That doesn't sound so bad," I said, puzzled by his apparent horror. What was there in commenting about things that made a coat rack look shell-shocked?

He gazed at me with a haunted expression. "She's *very loud*."

This clarified nothing—but clarity was coming down the hall. The distant voices were growing, and now I was sure I could hear a woman's voice. I automatically leaned out of my portrait, trying to make out words.

I needn't have bothered, as they grew increasingly audible. "Ooh, what a lovely mirror! It frames my face so perfectly! And the gold makes my hair glow. My mother told me I should always wear gold—it sets off my skin tone. I don't know, though, sometimes I think a little silver for accent is *just* the thing. Don't you agree?"

There was the barest rumble of a response, lasting for perhaps a quarter-second, before the woman's voice resumed.

"But really what I like is diamonds—and rubies! And *ooh*, look at this funny suit of armor! How could anyone walk around like that? Their face wouldn't show. And it's not flattering to the figure. I have always been noted for my figure. It's better than any woman I know. You can bet I keep an eye out. And *I* bet you noticed when I arrived! Ooh, what's through this door?"

Archambault made a frantic gulping sound and dove behind one of the several armchairs dotting the library. Quillsby fluttered his way up to perch on the edge of my frame. Mere seconds later the tall doors of the library swung silently open.

"*Ooh*, a library!" a very, very loud and high-pitched voice exclaimed. And there stood the woman from the lawn, the woman who had come to the castle and was our best hope for breaking this terrible curse. I'd forgive her the loud voice, the bright pink dress that clashed with her hair as much as the purple one, everything, if she broke the curse.

And maybe that exclamation had meant she was excited about a library. That would be a good sign.

"This is my favorite room," the Prince said in a low rumble. I had never heard him say before that he was fond of the library, despite the great lengths I had gone to encourage him in during earlier, happier days. He had come in so rarely since the curse struck (fortunately, considering the way he treated the books!) that I was still not used to his new form, seven feet tall and broad shouldered, with horns adding at least an extra six inches to his height. Not to mention the fur. That was also hard to get used to.

Despite his size, His Highness didn't entirely block the sight of Theodore, our butler-turned-armchair, awkwardly planted in the doorway. He was shifting back and forth as though he wanted to scurry away but didn't dare. I'd heard that the Prince had ordered Theodore to follow him around at all times, in case he needed somewhere to sit.

Meanwhile the woman was staring at the Prince, then suddenly went into a peal of laughter that echoed around the tower, rebounding and reverberating and knocking me back into the armchair in my painting. "Oh, you're so *funny*!" she squealed. "As if anyone's favorite room could be a *library*. Books are so *boring*."

About to introduce myself, I was shocked into silence, my painted skin crawling with horror. What sacrilege was this, spoken within the very walls of the library? What horrible kind of creature was this woman? Suddenly it seemed less strange that everyone else wanted to avoid her.

Quillsby flitted agitatedly along my frame, tracing lines in the accumulated pink dust, muttering to himself. "Well, I never. That is simply not—I do not approve—a lack of appropriate respect for the importance of letters is *not* what I call proper, not at all."

Over the top of Quillsby's feather, I watched the Prince inhale, chest expanding to an even greater size, while his furry hands curled into fists. Then he exhaled loudly, and in a low voice said, "I like books."

*I* heard the undercurrent of suppressed anger behind his words, even through my surprise at those words. The woman didn't seem to recognize his tone or care about what he had said. "Why does anyone need all this paper and stuff?" she prattled on. "It's not pretty, and you can't wear it, and it's not even valuable. I've been hearing all about your valuable castle my whole life, you know, and the stories only got grander after the place disappeared five years ago! So disappointing—I was only twelve, of course, but I had already planned out everything I could do with all the wealth in this big grand castle. I'm so *relieved* to have found the place after all. Now how much did you say you were worth?"

His Highness' anger seemed to have faded in the face of this long speech, though I guessed it was not soothed so much as outlasted. He just stared at her with his brow creased below his fur. "I don't know an exact amount," he rumbled.

"Oh well," she said, almost before he finished, "the castle alone must be worth a fortune. And all that lovely jewelry I saw earlier. And there must be a treasure vault. There *is* a treasure vault, yes?"

"There—"

"Of course, how silly, every castle has a treasure vault." She went into another peal of laughter that made the Prince flinch. "Oh, won't the girls back home be *jealous!* My mother always told me I was meant for great things. This is just what I deserve, and it's about time the right opportunity came along. Even if there's obviously a little bit of magic complicating things. Is this one of those curses where we have to get married to break your, you know, furry situation?"

The Prince was staring at her as though fascinated, but I don't think it was the good kind of fascination. I realized suddenly I was doing the same thing. I glanced around to see that Isadora and Quillsby were staring too, and I could just see the tip of Archambault's feather behind the armchair. Theodore had backed all the way out of the doorway, just the edge of one armrest still in sight.

"Breaking the curse," His Highness said finally. "That is—"

"Or is the answer not quite so cerebral?" The woman's smile took on an alarming gleam. "Does it take something a little more, you know, earthy? I don't mind if you don't. I'd do *a lot* for all that beautiful jewelry."

I was confused. I had read enough books that I felt I ought to know what she meant (psychology, west wall, shelves 22 through 28)—and Isadora had shunted off in the way that meant she was embarrassed, so perhaps she understood. If she did, I certainly ought to. But the Prince looked befuddled too, or at least he wasn't saying anything in the sudden silence.

Of course, the silence only lasted about four seconds anyway, before the woman put her hands on her hips, giggled and said, "Well, come on then. There's a couch right there." And she winked.

I caught her meaning then, and my confusion morphed into horror. Because I *couldn't leave*. At least Archambault and Quillsby could run away. I shrank down in my chair, covering my eyes with my hands.

"Oh my word," Quillsby muttered, "most improper, *most* improper!"

Fortunately for everyone in the room, His Highness somehow turned red through his fur and said quickly, "No, that's not the answer. No. Definitely not."

Another peal of laughter made my head hurt, but I was still profoundly relieved.

"Oh, very well," she said, in what was probably supposed to be a coquettish tone, and flounced off across the room. "I suppose a bit of romancing first, if you're shy."

I had never known the Prince to be shy, in any realm of life. Including this one, if rumors could be believed. In a way, I was surprised at his new reluctance. But on the other hand, considering this woman...

I didn't realize she was heading toward the harpsichord until she plopped down in front of it. "Really you ought to serenade me," she cooed, bringing her hands down on the keys in a discordant clang. "But I suppose I can sing for you. My mother always told me I had musical talent. I was simply meant to. That's why she named me Musette."

Then she sang. Loudly. Very loudly. And badly. *Very* badly.

I put my hands over my ears. It helped barely at all, and I felt for Isadora, who didn't even have hands. Quillsby leaped from my frame and fled out the library's door, and even Theodore had disappeared from sight.

That woman's voice was piercing, echoing all around the room and repeating on top of itself in an ever-rising cacophony of noise until I thought she was going to bring the entire place down around our ears. Or that the books would leap off the shelves and flee in protest.

And then a bellow cut across the noise, a bellow I had heard too many times and never before welcomed. "*Enough!*" the Beast roared—and he was, indeed, a Beast in this moment. With one huge paw he reached out and swept an entire shelf of books onto the ground in a thundering crash that made me flinch. "I will *not* listen to another moment of you and your wretched voice! I tried to control my temper—no one can say I didn't try—because I need you to break the curse, but I *can't* do this." Another crash as a second row of books was knocked to the floor. "Being polite is pointless. I don't care if your hair is an attractive shade, I don't *care* what you think you deserve, and I don't CARE about YOU! Get out!"

The echoes of the roar died away, and fortunately that woman had stopped singing. Musette stared at him for a moment in silent affront. Then she rose to her feet, head held high. "How dare you speak to me that way. Do you have any idea who I am? I'm the prettiest girl in my village, I'll have you know, and—"

"I will just have to settle for the second prettiest," the Beast growled, before seizing her arm and hauling her toward the door.

"IIow dare you!" she protested, stumbling after him. "You can't treat me like this. Let me go and apologize this instant, or I'm *leaving*!"

"So leave!" he shouted, and stormed out of the library, pulling Musette behind him.

A blessed quiet descended on the room. Very slowly I took a deep breath, and tapped one palm against my ear. I did still have my hearing. I had worried.

An anxious-looking feathered hat appeared above the back of the armchair. "Is she gone?" Archambault asked.

"I think she's going," I said. "I think he's throwing her out." For a moment I felt a surge of relief. And then disappointment. "So...she isn't going to break the curse."

"I don't think it was going to be true love anyway," Isadora remarked, sliding closer along the shelves. "And some things are worse than being cursed."

"No woman who hates books could be suitable," I agreed. "Her Majesty never would have accepted someone like that for her son." Considering that Queen Marie had been warm-hearted and accepting of very nearly everyone, whoever they were and wherever they came from, there were few condemnations I could make that would be worse.

I looked down at the tumbled pile of books on the ground, victims again of the Beast's rage, and slumped. "I don't see why he had to take his fury out on our poor books, though."

"We'll get Darwin to set them to rights again," Isadora said comfortingly. "And just think how much damage he would have done if she'd stayed longer and he'd grown even angrier."

"True enough," I said. If he had actually married her—I doubted a single book would have survived, and who knew about the rest of us? No, on the whole, this solution would have been worse than nothing. I tried to put the fallen books out of my mind for now. I leaned out of my frame, brushing the pink dust away, and plucked another book from the shelf. "Perhaps we can get down to a little good reading now."

# Chapter Four:
## Painting the Aftermath

In which the easel, piano, and quill wait because of ill-fated curses

**M**y hinges creaked as I turned toward where the grand piano, my dear Maximus, rested. How many times had I played out our wedding in my mind? I could have left this wretched place, lived and married as Madame Rebecca Stein; my own happily ever after.

But I didn't leave all those years ago. And now? We existed as pink dusted objects, waiting for the Beast to learn what he didn't seem to want to understand. We all took it in pained measure, but Maximus? He seemed less and less of the exuberant man he was and more a lost soul if there ever was an embodiment for such a thing.

He nimbly played on ghost ridden keys; it was a quiet tune and a personal favorite of mine for painting in the late afternoons. He must have realized I was watching because his music played with more vigor and performance. His eyes were no longer the gorgeous sea green that he was blessed with as a man, but the warm grains of the piano lumber still held his expressions. But, most days, his eyes were tired and worn with unfocused pupils. But, his confident play pulled my attention and I inched closer to listen. "That's quite beautiful, Maximus."

The music paused and his deep voice, richly layered with piano vibrato, said, "It's about you, you know."

I creaked the rest of the way over to where he rested in the study, and he rolled slowly in response. We stopped inches from each other and yet it was miles. I leaned forward, the edge of my canvas on the corner of his darkened cover. If I could dream while awake, then I would hold his hands in my own. How I longed to feel his touch, to steal the kiss he offered me as we planned to elope from this place. How I blamed myself for not leaving right as the words left his mouth, because of course I wanted to!

A sigh escaped as dust from the depth of my wooden frame, and gushes of paint whooshed across the blank canvas balanced across my middle; it erupted with wild color before settling into an image of a blue rose lost in a raging red volcano.

Maximus said with a shaking sound, "I feel the same way, my love."

Monsieur Quillsby floated in and whispered gently from the nearby credenza. "Mademoiselle Tempera, you must be more careful when you look at him." His feathers ruffled. "It is growing quite easy to determine your emotive state, my dear. And you must not let the Beast see you this way. You know how he gets."

Maximus rumbled, "Let him see! Let him see how he's ruined the lives of others! Let him know of the love he stole from us. It's been so long. I don't care to cater to him."

Monsieur Quillsby undeterred, huffed and said, "Well, you might try a little bit harder so we can all have a standing chance to leave this place! Granted, we are at odds you and I, most times, but I would much rather not see you broken because of a fit he chose to take out on you."

I straightened my wooden legs and relaxed to a more appropriate position for an easel. I cleared the canvas to a blank slate, only to have the image of broken love replaced with a graying sun, sparse and thin over the fabric. "Maximus, he's right, darling. We mustn't lose hope that—"

Maximus slammed his keys with a dissonant chord. "That what? That women such as the disaster that waltzed through here yesterday could possibly sway him into loving someone more than himself?" He grumbled and rolled away from me to his usual spot in place by the window. "No, I should think not."

Monsieur Quillsby whispered to where only I could hear, "What provoked Stein today?"

I wriggled the painting and finally the canvas remained empty. "Maximus has better days than others; today is not one of those days." Without meaning to, the likeness of his human form wandered over my mind and bled into the canvas. I could almost feel his brown hair and nimble fingers. I could almost see his long lashes and light eyes. I almost smelled his oaken scent and felt his warm touch on my shoulders.

"Ah, Mademoiselle Tempera, you might want to save that image for a more private moment, perhaps?" I looked down and saw that I had painted a portrait not of just Maximus, but of the two of us together locked in an embrace and lips parted inches from the other.

When the emotion cleared from my middle I said, "Of course, you are right. Which is why I have to limit my interaction with dear Monsieur Stein." My voice was different now, and often sounded as though my words rippled within the layers of variant brush strokes. I didn't altogether mind it, but sometimes it felt separate from me, as if it weren't even me at all.

Quillsby fluttered. "I don't know how you tolerate him after all these years."

The sadness built in paint again and I shook it violently away. "We are in love, Monsieur Quillsby. Have I told you that? Even after all this time, we ache in that love. He asked me to leave this place just before we were cursed." More images began to take shape over my canvas and I shook them away heartily and nearly shouted, "It is bad enough to be under a spell, but to have one's personal thoughts constantly on display? It can be downright humiliating."

Quillsby's feathers ruffled as though he were nodding and then he sneezed as the pink sparkles flitted in about what I presumed was his face. With as much dignity as a quill could manage, he adjusted himself and said, "Well, no one blames you for your emotions, dear." More flecks wound themselves within the curve of his feathers. "Oh those dastardly glitter specks are most invasive. Why that so-called good fairy felt the need to keep them here, I'll never understand." He roamed the large oak credenza and fluttered with conversation: "And why she cursed us as much as she cursed the Prince? Especially with all these dastardly glitterlings? They are most distracting and quite dangerous, you know." He sighed and wriggled a few extra sparkles from his feathers. "All of this was his wrong-doing, not ours."

Maximus spoke from his place in front of the window. "It doesn't matter why we were cursed, only that we were.

Every day, I watched the view hoping to see the one who will bring the cure for our conditions, but having only one deflated the dwindling hope I held onto. Besides, he doesn't seem to mind being a beast with how he still treats everyone. He has learned nothing."

Quillsby shook and shivered as he teetered this way and that, the way a feather might float on a breeze, until he found the inkpot seat he sought. He sat and mumbled half to himself, "Thankfully, not all of the objects are people. I would feel just awful if this inkpot was more than just an inkpot." He straightened and said to the both of us, "Well, did we expect anything different when that fairy came along? Have you seen how he makes Theodore follow him around simply because the poor dear was turned into a favorite sitting chair?"

I shivered as ravaged images of black clouds and a burned mountain spread across my canvas, sore from a rampage of intense heat. I left the image and whispered with a swishing sound, "If only the Prince could remember what it meant to be kind, like his mother taught him to be."

A rippling among the feather emulated a shake of the proverbial head, "It is most unsettling. Humiliating!"

Maximus, my dear love, was now silent. He rolled forward and backward in small pacing patterns. Sparkles swayed around his movement; constant reminders that magic was at play with our livelihoods.

I sighed and said, "I hope that the one true love will see past those things."

Maximus heard me and stopped his pacing. He spoke with deep chords before turning away from me, "Timing is everything."

My feelings filtered across the canvas before I could stop it; white flecks of hard rain blended over blue from the blackened soil before I quickly blanked the imagery. If Quillsby saw my sadness, he kindly chose to ignore it. He cleared his throat and shimmied away foreign sparkles that tried to cling to him.

Maximus said nothing, not even a grunted melody.

I shuddered as the same pink flecks kept grazing my wooden spine. "The Prince needs to understand what he has forgotten." My voice, a soft bristling, faltered for a moment as I thought of his mother and the cruel way the king treated the Prince after she died. I turned so as to face Monsieur Quillsby and said, "But how could he even understand unselfish love if he was so denied it after the Fair Queen died?"

Quillsby huffed as glitter abused his otherwise silky feather and then said, "Well, women like that monster who came to him will never teach him anything outside of what he already knows." He hunched over dramatically. "If that is all we have coming through, then—"

Maximus spoke up. "Then we are quite doomed to remain cursed."

I focused on the woman and created an intentional image across my canvas. "She was quite selfish, wasn't she?" I painted a version of the beautiful woman, and then distorted it with childish embellishments of what I envisioned the woman's true character: green skin and warts over her body.

Then, I painted the ghoulish woman holding a mirror who saw nothing but a blooming flower.

Quillsby laughed, a wind-like swoosh of a sound, and said, "Oh brilliant! Just brilliant, Mademoiselle."

The wood that housed my limbs creaked a bit as I leaned downward, an attempt to create a ladylike bow. "Thank you, thank you. I'll be here for all eternity." I tried to make light with the joke, but the reality of the word *eternity* sank deeply. I cleared the thought before they could see the dread that inevitably would show, and instead asked, "Do you think the right woman will find him?"

Quillsby's feathers fluttered as he said, "Well, only time will tell. Truth be told, I'm grateful he didn't choose that selfish one. If she stayed, she might keep the servants following her like objects, even if we were no longer, well, objects." He shivered. "No, I should say that while I am saddened to live without my human body, I would much rather be a glitter dusted quill than a servant to a woman like that."

My dear Maximus's frame tilted in such a way that indicated he was sleeping. He had grown more and more tired as the years waned on, which made me nervous. The curse affected our humanity all in different quantities it seemed, and while I was patient with it, Maximus was restless from the beginning. Oh, how he boomed his anger with loud symphonies and cantankerous melodies, but his desire to keep hold of his humanity sank deeper and out of sight. Yes, he was quiet now, and my heart mourned in the echoes of his silence.

I worked back to my favorite place in front of the window. The sun was at midday, and the grounds were somehow alive and lonely. I felt the scene paint rapidly across my chest, the colors winding gently over one another until the final product was the lone fountain centered in the middle with no water to please it. I shook the art away.

I could feel the artist that I was disappearing, slowly replacing my mind with that of a mere observer. What if we lost sense of our human souls altogether? What if a day came where I no longer worried about emotion fleeting across a blank canvas because a blank canvas was all I was left as?

# Chapter Five:
## Another Young Lady Arrives

In which a second visitor sets the castle musicians off-key

**"A**re you trying to get yourself smashed to bits?" I demanded, smacking Victor's violin bow away from his strings to stop him from playing. I'm a cello and my bow is bigger, and mightier. Though I would've preferred becoming a lute when that damned good fairy's spell cursed us all. Ladies loved the lute. Especially when I, Charles Melody, played it.

Victor leaned back, aghast, and then plucked up his bow and ran it across his e-string multiple times in retort.

"Don't use that tone with me," I told the Stradivarius. "I don't care how softly you were playing. The Beast has impeccable hearing." As Beasts do. "You know how he detests Vivaldi."

Victor played a couple notes.

"I'm not sure but I think a woman and a few bottles of Merlot had a lot to do with it. You know how those Italian fellows are." Personally, I believed the composer was overrated. Sure, his violin concertos were genius, but what about the cello? No one ever writes good concertos for the heavenly intonation of the cello. Or the lute.

"But that's not the point," I said, annoyed that Victor had managed to get me to go off on a tangent again. "No Vivaldi!"

"Now, Charles," Theodore, the Beast's favorite chair, called out from the entryway. "He was only trying to help brighten our spirits on this dark, gloomy day. I thought your playing was delightful, Victor, though I am partial to Bach."

"Yes, well, annoying the Beast won't help anything," I told the voiceless violin. "The rosebushes by the carriage house have finally started blooming again after his last outburst. So best keep silent when he's in the castle."

It had been years since a chance to break the curse had presented itself and the Beast was losing hope. Most nights he wandered the woods surrounding the estate alone. Plus, the pink and gold sparkles were spreading. Bits and pieces showed up in the oddest places and stuck to the Beast's fur. He often left glittering footprints all along the front hall.

Victor responded with a high-pitched little melody.

"Your sass is unappreciated."

A creak echoed through the main hall, causing Victor to stop playing. One of the front doors slowly opened, taxing the rarely used hinges. Victor and I peered around the doorway to see what was going on.

A young woman stepped in sideways, the panniers of her dress too wide to enter straight on. Clearly a woman of high fashion. "Hello? Is anybody home?" She gently closed the door before turning to gaze around the large foyer. "I'm sorry for barging in but I'm afraid I'm lost. Is there anyone here who can assist me?"

"It's a girl!" I whispered. Victor's bow ran across his strings excitedly before I could stop him. "Shhh! Do you want to scare her away?"

"Is someone there?" the girl asked, stepping further into the hall towards the room where we hid. "I need help." The bottom of her green dress was coated with mud and ripped in many places. Dirt smudged her face with tear trails running down her cheeks.

"Now look what you did," I told Victor as I pushed him back to the wall just as the girl entered our room. If we stayed perfectly still and silent, maybe she wouldn't notice us.

She gazed about, her brow wrinkled. "I could've sworn I heard something…" She strolled around the room dragging her hand behind her, fingers brushing over the wall and then across my fingerboard. I shuddered and barely stifled a moan. It had been too long since a woman had touched my strings.

After finding the room apparently empty, she shrugged and went back into the main hall. We carefully resumed our place, peeking around the door to watch her.

"She's very beautiful," I whispered to Victor. Her mahogany-colored hair was pulled up in a messy bun with random strands and leaves sticking out all over. Her skin glistened and her deep brown eyes shone bright with wonder; reminiscent of the state in which I left my lovers. The way she bit her bottom lip as she gazed around the great hall struck a chord deep within me. Please, let her be a cellist.

The familiar vibration of the Beast descending the staircase shot straight to my heart. With his mood lately, how would he react to a stranger barging into his home, uninvited? Would he remember his manners?

"Who are you? What are you doing here?" the Beast growled as he glared at the young woman from half-way down the stairs. His claws dug into the banister, a sign that he was annoyed. He must've heard Victor playing.

The woman's eyes widened as she backed away. "I-I...I'm sorry to bother you but I seemed to have gotten lost in the woods." She bumped into the front door and stopped. "I c-came upon your castle and hoped to find a place to stay until the morning." Her hand fumbled to find the doorknob behind her. "I'm sorry to bother you." She found the knob and swung the door open to leave when a bolt of lightning cracked across the sky. Thunder shook the ground as rain plunged from the dark clouds hovering overhead. She stood in the open doorway, gawking at the rampaging storm as rain pelted her face.

How I missed the sharp scent of a thunderstorm...and the delicate scent of a woman's skin after an active night. Ah, I would never take my olfactory sense for granted again.

"I thought you were leaving," the Beast's voice boomed in the vast entryway. A snarl curled his lips as he stared at her shivering form.

She glanced back, her perfect pearly-white teeth already chattering. She nodded. My heart broke for the young woman as she squared her shoulders and pushed the door open wider to accommodate her wide dress.

Just as she stepped over the threshold, the Beast blared, "On second thought," stopping her in her tracks. He drew in a deep breath. "It is far too dangerous for anyone to travel in this weather. You may stay here until the storm passes."

The woman glanced back and forth between the Beast and the storm, hesitant to make a move in either direction. Her indecision made me so tense I thought I'd pop a string.

Finally, after a moment, she closed the door against the thrashing winds. "Thank you. I appreciate your hospitality."

The Beast approached her, causing her to suck in a breath and tense up. Her gaze never left him as he stopped right in front of her. "You may help yourself to anything in the kitchen for supper and sleep in any available chamber. But the East Wing is forbidden," the Beast said.

"Why is it for—"

"It just is!" he bellowed, swiping off a random pink sparkle from his shoulder and glaring east. For some unknown reason, the pesky sparkles were accumulating so rapidly in that part of the castle that the Beast had ordered the wing closed to keep them contained. It wasn't working.

She gasped at the outburst, but then slowly let out her breath as the Beast stepped back, giving her some space. "All right," she said. "No going into the East Wing."

The Beast suddenly seemed unsure of himself as he glanced at the floor. Was he losing his confidence?

Victor gently ran his bow across his strings in an encouraging little tune. The Beast inclined his head toward the room we were hiding in, a frown on his face, before straightening his shoulders and holding out a paw to the woman. "Would you like to join me for dinner?"

The woman also glanced toward where Victor quietly played, but then snapped her attention back to the Beast and his proffered paw. She stared at what used to be human hands, her gaze traveling up his thick arms until she reached his face. "Oh, uh, yes," she said, slowly placing her hand in his. "I would be honored."

As they walked to the dining hall, the girl kept glancing about. "Do you hear music?"

"No," the Beast said, glaring into the room as they passed, silencing the little violin. But as soon as they were out of earshot, we struck up a happy jig. Excited whispers swept through the castle. "She stayed. She must be the one!"

While the Beast allowed the girl to freshen up before dinner, Victor and I made our way to the dining hall and hid in the darkest corner to watch. Two plates were already set at the long dining table when the Beast and his enchanting guest entered. Piles of fresh, hot food sat in the middle, ready to be served. With such short notice of company, the kitchen had probably cooked up everything they had to impress the girl. The serving dishes had also sneaked into the room and hid in the shadows to watch. Everybody's future depended on this woman.

The Beast's gaze wandered over the table as he tugged at the collar of his shirt. He hadn't used utensils to eat in years, preferring to use his paws because it was easier. He'd had no one to impress for a long time. Again, Victor played a little melody of encouragement as the Beast reached out to take the soup ladle. He couldn't wrap his rather large fingers around the slender handle, nearly spilling the tomato bisque all over the white linen tablecloth.

The girl smiled and rescued him before he could spill and served the soup up in both of their bowls. They slurped their soup in silence for many uncomfortable minutes. Victor played again, a happy tune to set the mood.

"So, uh…" the Beast started.

"Angeline," the girl said with a crooked smile while she scooped up the roasted vegetables onto their plates.

"Angeline," the Beast said as if trying out the taste her name. "Why were you in the forest alone? Do you live in the village across the river?"

She frowned as she set the serving spoon back into the bowl. "Not yet. I was supposed to marry the man I *thought* loved me and move to the town but apparently, I was mistaken." She took a bite of a carrot and chomped hard on the poor root.

"Oh," the Beast said, his timbre deflating. "You are engaged." He grabbed the goblet of red wine at his side and downed it in one gulp. "I'm so happy for you," he said dryly as he set the glass down a little too hard.

The servants all slumped in our hiding spots. Her heart already belonged to another. Victor's bow slid off his strings in a disappointed slur.

"Not anymore," she said, biting hard on a brussels sprout. She waved her fork in the air as she said around her food, "He isn't the man I thought he was. The wedding is off."

We all perked back up, leaning in a little closer to hear better. "Oh? What happened?" the Beast asked, absently chewing his food while she had his full attention. His tail wagged excitedly from side to side as he listened.

"I don't want to talk about it," Angeline said as she speared another sprout. After a few minutes she had cleaned her plate and gazed over at his. "Are you going to eat that?" she asked, pointing her fork at his roasted potato. He slid his plate closer to her, so she could help herself.

"Why are men never satisfied with one woman?" she asked before taking a bite. "Why do they feel the need to stray? Especially right before they are to be married?" She swallowed hard and then looked at the Beast. "Am I not pretty enough?"

"Yes! I mean no," the Beast said quickly. "I mean…" He leaned back into his chair. "You are lovely and any man who doesn't see that is a fool."

The girl smiled at the Beast. "Thank you. You're so kind. Inviting a perfect stranger into your lovely home and listening while she rants about her no-good fiancé." She shook her head. "*Former* fiancé," she corrected.

The candelabra next to me nearly burned my scroll as his flames flared in excitement while the young woman fumed over her misfortune. I could practically feel the curse lifting already. Victor couldn't help himself as he played a few lively notes.

"Do you hear that?" the girl asked, setting her fork down as she squinted into the darkness.

I bumped Victor with my bow. "Silence," I whispered. He was going to ruin everything. If she knew the castle was cursed, she might flee before she could fall in love.

"No, uh…" the Beast scrambled to distract her. He grabbed a platter and held it out to her. "Would you like some roast duck?"

She stared at it in silence. After a moment, the Beast set the food down, uncertainty clouding his face as he watched her eyes water. "Philippe is the best duck hunter in the village," she choked out as tears streamed down her face.

She grabbed her napkin and held it to her eyes while sobs wracked her body.

The Beast watched, wide-eyed as she cried. He glanced over to the shadows to where we sat, silently pleading for help. None of us knew what to do with a weeping girl.

"I thought...he l-loved me," she sobbed into the cloth.

Victor sniffed and played a melancholy tune while she wept, tears rolling down his fingerboard.

"Don't encourage her," I admonished, wiping away a tear of my own. Who knew being a cello for so long would make me so soft?

After minutes of weeping, Angeline straightened up and blew her nose. "I'm so sorry," she said, dabbing the moisture from her eyes. "I'm not usually one for such outbursts. You've been nothing but kind to me and I ruined such a lovely meal with my despondency."

"That's perfectly fine," the Beast said, flinching as she blew her nose into her napkin again. Lightning flashed just outside the castle and lit up the dining room. Rain had continued to pour.

In the corner, Victor played a soft lullaby. The Beast said nothing as he stared at the sniffling girl. Why wasn't he saying anything? This curse wasn't going to break itself. I reached out tentatively and tapped the Beast with my bow. Praying that he wouldn't bite my scroll off for my forwardness, I whispered, "Invite her to stay the night."

He turned his head slightly, tossing me a glare but then said, "The storm doesn't appear to be letting up. It's too dangerous to be out in such a torrential downpour. I can show you to a bedchamber you may use for the night."

"Oh?" she asked between sniffs. She glanced behind her, out the giant window to see the wind thrashing trees in the surrounding forest and the rain rolling down the glass panes. She shivered. "I suppose you're right." She looked at the Beast and gave him a watery smile. "Thank you."

He stood and offered his arm, which she took without hesitation. Victor could barely keep still as we all watched the Beast lead the young woman up the main staircase to one of the empty chambers.

"Did you see that?" the dishes clinked excitedly. "She likes him. She's the one!"

"Don't count your notes before they've been played," I said. "It takes more than one kind gesture to fall in love." Once the dishes had gathered up the food and clamored back into the kitchen, I leaned in closer to Victor and whispered, "I think she's the one!"

The next morning, Victor and I played a lively little tune while the other servants danced in joy in the great room. Excitement filled the air. We were so close to breaking the curse and returning to our true forms. I couldn't wait to waltz on two legs again, with that lovely buxom dairy maid, Frostine, in my arms. Even the Beast almost smiled at the scene as he ordered everyone to get back to work before the girl heard us celebrating.

When Angeline did finally emerge from her chamber in the late morning, her eyes were red and puffy. She stepped lightly down the stairs, hand gliding down the freshly polished banister. Everyone had worked all night to make the castle gleam in hopes of impressing her. The gardening shears had even gone out of his way to find the prettiest flowers in the garden to brighten the hallway.

The girl stopped at the table with the large vase full of the brightest purple irises in the countryside. She reached out and gently rubbed one of the petals with her delicate fingers. The corner of her mouth pulled up into a smile. "These are lovely," she whispered. "Almost as beautiful as the flowers Philippe offered when he first started courting." She bit her bottom lip as it trembled, and water filled her eyes.

"She's not going to cry again, is she?" Robert, the shaggy mop, asked as he peered around the corner to the hall. "She was sniffling all night. At this rate, I'll have to follow her around just to clean up her tears."

"She's been through a lot," I said. "Give her some time to get over that fool. Then she'll see what a catch the Beast is." Hopefully he wouldn't lose his temper and scare her away.

Before the tears could fall, the girl wiped her eyes and straightened her shoulders. She strode to the dining hall, fresh determination lighting her face. Victor played a couple sassy notes as she walked away.

The Beast joined her for breakfast. A few of us peeked through the opening of the French doors leading to the dining room to watch. They chatted in lively fashion with each other about the various tapestries hanging on the walls while they ate. She seemed to be enjoying his company if her smiles were any indication. At least until she chomped down on her toast and mulberry jam. She paused, slowly chewing as she set the rest down on her plate. A moment later she burst into tears. "Philippe is allergic to mulberries," she said around the lump in her throat. "One bite could kill him."

"She's crying again," Archambault, the coat rack, said, his arms drooping. "You'd think she'd be dehydrated by now."

"We need to cheer her up," I said, hopping back and forth on my endpin in front of the dining room doors. "Get her mind off that fiancé of hers." But what could we do without revealing ourselves? She was already in such a delicate state, we might push her over the edge.

Victor stroked his strings.

I glared at the little violin. "We are *not* going to send the man mulberries."

Footsteps approached the door, sending the other servants scrambling to avoid being seen. I flattened myself against the wall as best I could, nearly getting hit with the door as the Beast escorted the sniffling girl into the hall.

"Would you like a tour of the castle?" the Beast asked gruffly. I was impressed he hadn't thrown her out already with her near constant crying.

She sniffed and wiped at her nose with a lacy handkerchief. "That would be lovely."

He led her to the library.

"Let's hope Philippe isn't a big reader," Robert said, sliding over to the bookcase to rest.

"The poor girl is surely doing her best," I told everyone, waving my bow around. "I'm sure the Beast will chase away any lingering feelings she may still harbor for that no-good scoundrel in no time." At least I hoped so. I would love to see her smile again.

The Beast emerged from the library, alone. A frown pulled at the corners of his mouth as he stomped down the stairs. "Did you know that Philippe's brother's wife's sister knows this man who married the fourth cousin thrice removed of Shakespeare's tailor?" He fell back into Theodore, trusting his favorite chair would be there to catch him. The Beast clenched his fists as he glared into the roaring flames in the hearth. "We must burn all his sonnets."

I snickered. Hugo the librarian would never stand for it.

The Beast stood and approached the fireplace, gripping the mantel while hunched over in thought. Those of us in the room remained still and quiet, not daring to disturb him. He tensed up right before roaring so loudly the chandeliers rattled. He cleared everything off the mantel in one swipe of his paw, glass and metal crashing to the floor. He stomped out of the castle, retreating to the woods as we all quickly cleaned up the mess before the girl could find it. I hoped she would get over this Philippe fellow soon, before the Beast's tantrums broke everything.

For the next couple days, we all followed Angeline around, at a distance, cleaning up the discarded handkerchiefs she littered throughout the castle as every little thing reminded her of her precious Philippe. Even Victor had grown tired of her tears, repeating a dark, ominous motif whenever she drifted out of earshot.

"I don't know what else to do!" The Beast slammed his fists down on the arms of his chair, causing poor Theodore to flinch. Victor and I had wandered in, hoping to offer inspiration with a melody. "I invited her to stay at the castle as long as she'd like. She is beautiful, educated, and refined. I could build a life with her, curse or no curse. But everything she sees reminds her of Philippe; the chandelier, the pattern on the rug in her bedchamber, even that damn fairy's sparkles reminds her of the way his golden hair shines in the sunlight." He flexed his fingers to expose his sharp claws. "If I ever meet this Philippe, I will tear him apart limb from limb for making me endure the very mention of his name. Repeatedly."

"She will get over him," I assured him while Victor gently played in the background. If she accepted his offer, maybe I could teach her all about the wonders of playing a cello. I could instruct her on how to properly hold a bow and stroke it across my strings.

A sob slipped under the doorway, coming from the hall. The Beast sighed and rolled his eyes before standing. "I should make sure she's all right," he said as he shuffled to the door. He stopped, one paw on the handle. "I'm not sure there is room enough in her heart for me, too."

"Oh," Angeline said as soon as the Beast came into view, dabbing at her nose and eyes to clear the tears. "I was looking for you." She forced a smile on her delicate face. "I have thought about your proposal and I'd like to accept."

Excitement lit up my hollow body and the urge to play a roaring song sung through my bow. She'd agreed to stay with the Beast. Would that satisfy the curse?

The Beast stood straighter as he grinned. "You'll be very happy here. I promise you."

She nodded, lips pressed into a thin line as fresh tears welled up. "I'm sure I will be."

I stood still, breath held, waiting for sparkles to whip up into a frenzy and turn us all back to our former glory. I couldn't wait to have my old body back. To eat again. To play my lute again. To woo that lovely little Frostine in the kitchen. She had always saved the very best croissant for me at breakfast.

The Beast fidgeted as he stood in front of her, glancing all around, obviously waiting for something magical to happen too.

A loud pounding on the door interrupted the awkward silence. The door creaked open and a blond man peered inside. "Hello? Is anybody…?" His gaze fell on the girl and he pushed himself inside. "There you are!" He ran to her and wrapped her up in his arms. "I've been searching all over for you," he said into her silky hair.

"This must be Philippe," I whispered to Victor. I had to hold my little friend back from attacking the man with his bow. Whether to avenge his treatment of the girl or to get revenge for making us endure endless stories of him, I wasn't sure.

She pushed the man away and stepped closer to the Beast, whom he apparently hadn't noticed until just then, if the way his eyes widened was any indication. "I'm surprised you even realized that I was gone," she said snidely.

"This will be fun," I whispered to Victor as we watched from the parlor. "A woman scorned and all."

Philippe pulled out a dagger from his side sheath and pointed it at the Beast. He grabbed the girl by her wrist and pulled her away and behind him. "Are you all right? Did he steal you away?" He was either extremely brave or extremely stupid. My money was on the latter.

"I'm quite all right," she clipped as she pulled away from the man and then walked to the Beast's side. "And no, he did nothing of the sort. I got lost in the forest when the storm hit, and the Beast was kind enough to offer me shelter. He has taken excellent care of me and has even invited me to stay permanently." Her eyes narrowed as she glared at the man. "And I accepted."

"Accepted?" The man staggered back, the arm holding his dagger falling back to his side. "To stay with this...this...monster?" Disgust distorted his handsome face as he sneered at the Beast. He brandished his dagger again, eyes narrowed. "He probably plans to eat you."

A low growl came from the Beast as he stared down the man, rising to his full height. His knuckles popped as he clenched his fist. Really, if the Beast wanted to eat her, he'd be picking his teeth with her bones by now.

"Besides," Philippe continued, his gaze shifting back to the girl. "You belong with me."

"I belong with you?" The girl laughed. "Are you sure it is I you want to marry? Not Elizabeth?"

"Elizabeth?" Confusion wrinkled Philippe's brow as his attention bounced back and forth between her and the Beast. "Why would I...?" Realization dawned on him as he focused solely on her. "There is nothing between her and me beyond acquaintance. I was merely helping her with her horse."

"Is that what they call it?" I whispered to Victor.

The girl's resolve slipped ever so slightly at his revelation, but she schooled her features before saying, "That isn't what it looked like when I saw you with her in the stables."

Philippe placed his palm to his chest, the presence of the Beast apparently no longer a threat as he spoke. "I swear to you that there is nothing between that woman and me and there never will be. You are the only one for me. My heart will shrivel up and die if you do not return with me now."

I could feel the chance to break the curse slipping through my strings the longer the girl watched him plead his love for her.

The Beast turned to the girl. "I can offer you everything you could ever want," he said, taking her delicate hands. "There is nothing I would ever deny you. You would be very happy here."

Philippe dropped to his knees. "I cannot offer you the riches that this beast can. But I can promise that I will dedicate my life, nay, my *soul* to your happiness."

She slipped her hands free of the Beast's hold and then wandered over to the ornate mirror. She watched her reflection, slipping a stray curl behind her ear as doubt warred in her eyes. Who would she choose?

"You'll learn to love the Beast," Archambault said as he leaned in closer, the weight of the enormous feather tipping his hat forward.

The girl jumped back. "Who said that?" She stared at the coat rack and his pink fur coat before her gaze drifted over the hall. She stepped backwards, pointing accusingly at the rack. "I keep hearing voices. Whispered voices in empty rooms. And music playing. This castle is haunted."

The Beast shrugged. "Enchanted, actually…"

Philippe placed his hands on her shoulders as soon as she was within arm's reach. "I heard it, too. Let me take you home," he said as he turned her around to face him. "I will keep you safe."

"Oh, Philippe," she whispered and then threw her arms around him. He picked her up and carried her out of the castle and into the forest, never to be seen by any of us again.

The Beast fell back into Theodore, his shoulders slumped as he ran a paw down his face. "That could've gone better."

I peeked out of the window in hopes that she had changed her mind, but she was gone. So much for our music lessons.

# Chapter Six:
## Surely the Next One...

In which the kitchen dreams of better days

"What's on the menu tonight?" Samuel the stove asked to the kitchen staff at large. He sparked up a large flame inside his oven in anticipation.

We'd all been so excited to cook for people again since the weeping young woman appeared days ago. Not that I do any of the cooking, of course. Iceboxes don't have the right equipment. "Anything will do," I said. "As long as it has cheese in it. I'm practically overflowing with the stuff." Dealing with dairy wasn't new to me as I was the dairy maid before that wretched good fairy drowned the castle in those pesky sparkles.

"Oh, Frostine," Marthe the mixer said to me. "How we French love our fromage."

"Do you think she'd like a nice fondue?" Samuel asked. The pots and pans hanging from the rack above him rattled as a couple fell from their hooks and landed on his burners.

"She might." I tossed out the fromage and vegetables that had a few good days left onto the cutting board. "At least it will use up all this food." The knives snapped to attention and chopped up the produce and a nice baguette while Samuel got the cheese ready. The mix of wine and cheese swirling around the kitchen filled me with happiness. Before the curse, our chefs were known for their delicious dishes of duck l'orange, coq au vin, and boeuf bourguignon.

But when we were only feeding the Beast, he desired less our fancy culinary feats and eventually preferred simpler dishes and the occasional steak tartare. The young woman's presence had sparked our creative juices again and brought us back to life, so to speak.

"I'll whip up a crème brûlée for dessert," Marthe said as her beaters spun. "It was one of the Queen's favorites."

"Calm down, Marthe," Rouge the black tea towel said as she whirled around the mixer, cleaning up the splatters coming from her bowl. "You're making a mess to rival the one in the East Wing."

The kitchen door swung open just as the little tune the dishes started humming had spread to the napkins and candlesticks. Quillsby fluttered in and halted our joyous moment when he shouted, "She's gone!"

Only the sound of bubbling cheese could be heard after that. "What do you mean she's gone?" I asked, not wanting to believe that our usefulness could be over so soon. "But she just got here." It had only been a few days. We hadn't even gotten to cook the escargot yet.

Quillsby raced further inside and waited for the silverware to crowd around him, ready to hear the story. "That Philippe fellow barged into the castle and whisked her away, even after she agreed to stay with the Beast."

"Philippe?" I asked. "The one she's been crying over since she got here? The one who broke her heart?" Why would she give someone who hurt her so badly a second chance?

"Oh, you should have seen it," Quillsby said, hopping up on top of Marthe so the rest of the kitchen could hear him better. "That scoundrel burst through the main doors, calling out for the girl. As soon as he saw the Beast, he brandished his sword and challenged him to a duel."

The little teacups gasped in unison. "No!"

"Yes!" said Quillsby with a wave of his plumage. "He charged at the Beast, and would have run him through if not for the Beast's quick reflexes. Philippe parried and thrust, chasing the Beast around the great hall while the girl could do nothing more than cry in the corner."

Of course, she was crying. But for whom? "Is the Beast all right?" I asked. Would the curse continue if he died? What would become of us?

"The Beast is unharmed. At least physically," Quillsby said. "Watching the girl willingly leave with that man after everything he had done for her wounded his pride and his heart."

"How could she leave with him after what he did to her?" I asked, opening my door to let a lagging carrot back into my cold box. "From what the China told me, he was rolling in the hay with another woman." Literally.

"He denied any wrongdoing, wooing her back into his good graces. The blaggard!" Quillsby slumped slightly as his ire diminished. "She didn't even say goodbye as he whisked her off back to the village, leaving our Beast heartbroken and the curse intact."

The lively mood in the room melted away, leaving heavy hearts. Sam extinguished his flame and the cutlery trudged back into their drawers. "So much for dinner," Marthe said sadly, turning off her beaters.

Charles the cello waddled into the kitchen just as the cut vegetables returned to my shelf. "The girl has...Oh, I see you've already heard," he said as his gaze fell upon Quillsby on the counter.

"Yes, I've already informed the kitchen staff." The bright white quill hopped off the counter and toward Charles, practically shoving the cello out of the door. "Let us go chat with the chambermaids in the West Wing."

"I can't believe the Beast almost died!" Rouge said, folding into herself.

"Died?" Charles asked, glancing down at the quill pushing against him. He stood his ground, not budging. "What exactly did you tell them?"

"I told them that the girl was gone. Is she not? Now, about the chambermaids..." Quillsby tried to hop past the cello, but Charles's bow stopped him in his tracks.

Charles looked to me. "What have you heard, mon cherie?"

If I still had blood running through my veins, I would be blushing. Instead, I said "It must have been quite frightening to witness the Beast being chased around the hall by a crazy man and his sword."

"What sword?" Charles asked, glancing sideways at Quillsby. "Do you mean that puny little dagger? No, there was no fight. That Philippe fellow found the girl and explained away the misunderstanding. But when he asked her to leave with him, she first refused, planning to honor her promise to the Beast. Until that big mouth Archambault spoke and alarmed the girl." Charles sighed at the memory.

"Yes, yes," Quillsby said, hopping in front of the cello. "And because of that, no one must ever speak to another human to come to the castle again. We can't afford to frighten off any more women until this curse is broken. I can barely remember what it feels like to have hands to write with."

"Indeed," I said, straining my brain to remember what I looked like in my human form. I knew I was a slender yet strong woman, the perfect height to milk the cows every day. But the features of my face were getting hazier. I knew I had a beauty mark, but exactly where it was seemed to change on a daily basis. If the curse wasn't broken soon, I might never recall my face again. "May the next woman come swiftly. Before it's too late."

# Chapter Seven:
## Yet Another Young Lady Arrives

In which a third visitor fails to value the finer things in life
— like books

O nce I was known as Lady Jayne Beatrice Anne
Smythe. I thought. After all these long years,
sometimes I was no longer sure. Lately, I feared
my memory had been failing, just like everything else
around here.

Though I came from noble blood, I was penniless when
Papa died; he left me with nothing but loneliness and grief.
Fortunately, Queen Marie never judged others by class or
circumstance. I'd have starved in a British gutter if not for
her. After she brought me to France, we became close. I
gladly cared for her books and papers, keeping her organized
and on time, and she told me often how much I was
appreciated. She was such a beautiful soul.

So unlike her son.

Even when sickness trapped her in bed, I had seen to her
comfort. And at the end, she begged me to care for the
Prince when she was gone. Even though I never liked him,
how could I refuse her final request?

When she died, I was left alone again. I bitterly regretted
my promise over the years. I stayed, though I no longer had
a real place. Still, I hoped I could turn the Prince from his
self-destructive path. And I did try, truly. But he never
listened — not to me, not to anyone.

"Has it been forty years, or fifty?" I asked, not willing to trust my memory.

And Moll Flanders, my dearest friend, said, "I am a book, not a calendar. But to answer your question, I believe it has been closer to fifty."

Trapped as a bookcase for fifty years, just because our prince was a thoughtless, spoilt young man. I'd never approved of his behavior before that nasty fairy came. No gentlewoman could be comfortable with his excesses. I only wished he was more like Queen Marie than his class-conscious father. Then, perhaps, we might not have been in this predicament. Though some servants didn't expend much effort to curb his dissipations, none deserved this.

When His Ungrateful Highness decided the Queen's old office would make an amiable game room for his wild revelries, he demanded Her Majesty's books be removed. Many had duplicates in the castle library, and he ordered me to do away with them, over my strenuous objections. Which was why I was in the hallway leaning against an old bookcase, my eyes nearly blinded with tears, my arms filled with leather-bound volumes, when that sparkly pink creature cast her evil spell. It took mere moments for my body to shift, turning hard and wooden, while all those books settled neatly into place on my shelves.

And there I've stood all these long, tedious years.

The first few decades weren't so bad as I enjoyed the various fictional narratives. Though the curse had trapped me, it somehow freed the books on my shelves. They became gifted with speech and gladly shared their stories: dashing Don Quixote, adventurous Gulliver, my daring Moll

Flanders, all the glorious works of Mr. Shakespeare. So many tales of chivalry and daring and true love.

In the beginning, I believed some young woman would come and break the curse. It even seemed romantic, like tales of star-crossed lovers who manage to find a way. I was disappointed when the first proved so obviously unsuited to be the lady of the castle. The second might have been a good match, but didn't work out either. There hadn't been the slightest sign of True Love with either of them. The first he couldn't bear, while the second he merely tolerated.

Moll Flanders and I spoke often of love, though she did not believe in True Love. Which struck me as quite peculiar - she'd married so very often.

Our conversations rambled for hours, mostly because Moll used ten words where one would do. And she described her life in Capital Letters: "The Fortunes and Misfortunes of the Famous Moll Flanders Who was born in Newgate prison and during a life of continued Variety, for Twelve Years a Whore, five times a Wife, Twelve Years a Thief, Eight Years a Transported Felon in Virginia, at last grown Rich, lived Honest and died a Penitent."

"How can you of all people not believe in true love?" I asked today.

"I believe in being cared for by one who professes love," Moll said, and gave a bawdy laugh.

I was disturbed. Not that she'd laugh at such a sentiment, though I failed to see the humor. No, it was that her laugh was not as strong as when our long enchantment had begun.

Moll had become my dearest friend over the years. She put up with my oft-voiced complaints of being trapped in the hall by the main doors, witness to all that happened here. She frequently scolded, "Don't be ridiculous, Jayne. It is like watching stories come to life. Be grateful. We could be stuck in some dark corner, reduced to watching spiders spinning their webs."

Which always made me laugh, and cemented our unlikely friendship.

I suppose it was not particularly strange to lose track of how long we'd been trapped like this. Not if Moll was right and it had been fifty years. Did anyone remember our existence? What chance was there of any girl, let alone the *right* girl, showing up? Perhaps Moll was correct and True Love only existed in books. Perhaps there would be no happily ever after, for any of us.

For some, it was already too late. Over the years, as the various stories within my books had been told and retold, and as more of those itchy pink sparkles drifted onto their spines, many of my books fell silent. As if their magic had been sucked back out from them. One after another, they turned to mere paper and cloth, and I felt each loss. Though I didn't mind so much when Hamlet stopped talking; he was always filled with gloom. And Juliet had been worse in her way. I was grateful when she finally stopped complaining about her short, sad life. After all, she'd had True Love and thrown it, and her Romeo, away.

Some might argue that we weren't really living at this point. But I could still think, so I believed I must live.

Besides, I hoped I would never feel utter mortification after death. So many forgot that I could see and hear *everything* in this hallway. I'd been forced to witness tragedies and the most private of sentiments.

Like His Beastly Highness. He had been growing desperate. Stalking up and down the hallways, just as he was doing now. "...all these years and not one peep from that nasty little fairy," he growled as he drew near. "If she was here right now, I'd rip her wings off and stuff them..."

He paced away, and I lost a few words before he turned back, gesticulating in agitation, lips pulled back from long, sharp teeth. "...servants grow mutinous and stare at me with contempt. As if any of them could find love with that fashion obsessed female or that completely lovesick young lady. But they care not for logic. They stare at me when they think I don't see, and their eyes demand the impossible!"

He paused before me, head hanging low, voice suddenly rough and...desolate? "After so long, everyone is losing hope. Well, so am I. How can I be expected to find love with just any girl who decides to show up? It is ridiculous!"

Once again, he turned and stalked away, but this time he kept going, leaving me to ponder what he'd said. Perhaps it wasn't fair to expect him to love the first or second girl to come along. But he was right about the servants; many were growing bitter to still be trapped in these useless forms.

"Hark! Something wicked this way comes," cried the 2nd Witch (*Macbeth*, Act 4, Scene 1).

"Don't be ridiculous," I snapped, then raised my voice, being extra friendly to make up for the unwelcoming Witch. "That's Robert."

I quite liked Robert.

"It's about time," Moll muttered. "There's sparkles piled up around your, ahem, bottom, Jayne."

He swept his way into the hall and came to rest beside me. Although swept was not, perhaps, the most accurate word. But mopped lacks...panache. Which Robert always had. He came often to polish the front hallway, and always made time to talk to me. Today, however his panache had deserted him. He panted out, "A young lady. Walking. Down the drive."

"Ah! I'm happy for you, Jayne," Moll said quietly.

"Don't forget how badly the last two ended," I cautioned.

"Third time's the charm, so they say," she told me, but instead of the stirrings of anticipation *I* felt, she sounded...sad. "Of course, it was the fifth time for me."

Before I could answer, the door was flung open. Robert let himself slump back against the wall.

Standing in the doorway was a young woman with a glorious head of curly blonde hair. She looked a bit rough around the edges; mud splashed high on her pale blue skirt, tatters along the hem. She must have walked for miles through our enchanted forest, but she still managed to hold a dainty smile on her face, her gracefully curved lips a delicate pink.

Her smile faded as she looked around the (apparently) empty hallway. In fact, I'd even describe her expression as a pout. "After a completely miserable journey to get here, to restore everything to its former glory, you would think the least His Highness could do is meet me at the door!"

She stepped over the threshold and glanced around, a delicate frown marring her beautiful features. She didn't let her eyes pause for a moment on my shelves, merely looked past, looked *through* all my lovely books as if they didn't exist. She turned to the great room across the hall and shook her head, making her thick curls dance upon her shoulders. "How hideous," she blurted.

Hideous? Had her mother not taught her better manners than that?

She took a step into the room, her delicate heels making ticking sounds on the elegant parquet floor, and added, "It looks as if my great-great grandmother decorated this place."

"And who might she be?" His Highness asked in his most restrained voice as he stalked into the hall. At least he wasn't trying to scare her off for being so insufferably rude. His expression was pleasant, if a beast's face can ever be called pleasant. And for the first time in a long time I felt a stirring of hope. She might be rude, but she'd come here to restore things.

"Oh!" She placed a delicate hand on her silk-clad bosom and fluttered her eyelashes. "You startled me, Your Highness. I didn't hear you come in."

He glanced down at his furred feet — he had the ability to stalk silent as a great cat when he chose — then looked back at the girl. "You seem to know who I am, and I'd very much like to know how. But first, what do I call you?"

"Juliette." She fluttered her eyelashes again. "My name is Juliette."

Oh no, another Juliet. Hopefully this one would have the good sense not to throw away True Love.

"I see," His Highness said affably. Well, *I* knew he was being affable. Too bad he looked so beastly when he smiled like that.

Juliette looked him up and down, then said, "You are obviously the one under a curse. We'll fix that. And you are not quite as hideous as I'd feared."

"You know about me." He said this softly as if to himself, then asked her, "How, exactly, did you learn of me? Of my castle?"

Juliette gave him a pretty smile but didn't bother fluttering her lashes this time. "Our nurse used to tell us the story of the enchanted castle and the lonely Beast who had to find someone to love. He would fall in love with a beautiful maiden, the curse would be broken, and they would live happily ever after." She looked back into the great room and grimaced briefly. Then she shrugged. "I always dreamed of being a grand lady and living in a castle, so here I am."

"Your father let you come? Based upon an old story?"

"Well, he doesn't know where I am." She didn't look the least bit worried by that admission. "He expects me to be meeting with that rich old merchant they want me to marry. Me. Marry a merchant!" She gave an affronted laugh. "My father is a Baron, a member of the aristocracy."

"Barely aristocracy," Robert whispered, just for me to hear. "Like *that* makes her important."

Juliette smiled at His Highness again, though it looked a bit forced. "I told him I would not be married off to some grubby old member of the bourgeoisie. All my older sisters got to marry an aristocrat. It's hardly my fault that Father only found eleven eligible bachelors." Her mouth tightened and she glanced down quickly as if to hide her expression. When she looked back up, her lips had curved into a sad, wistful smile. An irresistible smile.

His Highness resisted. In fact, he didn't even seem to notice. "You knew a Beast lived here, yet you came anyway?" He appeared dazed, shaking his great head from side to side.

"My sisters will all be insanely jealous. None married better than a Vicomte. I'll be royalty. I'll have royal parties!"

"Parties," His Highness muttered as his huge mane stood on end, like the hair along a cat's back. Unfortunately, that made the few sparkles caught in it this evening appear even more prominent.

"Of course, we'll have parties!" She looked him up and down and tapped her foot as the smile slid from her face. "Although, we really *must* do something about all that hair." She cocked her head, first to one side, then the other, staring at that tawny mane. "Yes, I intend to have lots of beautiful parties. I'll invite my sisters and watch them turn green with envy. They deserve that after all the teasing I received from them. I didn't choose to be the youngest and the prettiest of twelve sisters."

"I—"

"Don't worry," she continued, as if he hadn't started to speak, and I waited for an eruption that never came. I was sure she was trying for sweet and indulgent, but it was as cloying as an overly sweet croissant. "This room will be excellent for parties. Once we update the furnishings, of course. We'll stand at the top of those curving stairs, my hand resting on your arm until every eye is upon us." She looked back at His Highness and hesitated. "Well, maybe I'll come down alone, while you stare adoringly from down here."

She waved her hand at the great room. "I assume the rest of the castle is similar to this, yes?" She didn't wait for agreement. "It simply will not do."

"I... I realize there's a bit of dust." I had never heard His Highness sound so stiff, so formal. And I couldn't believe he was trying to pass off the fairy's sparkles as dust.

Beside me, Robert stirred and muttered, "It's not dust."

I whispered back, "I know!"

"No, no, it's not the dust, really," Juliette said. "Though what on earth have your servants been doing?" She didn't wait for an answer. "No, it's just...everything will have to go. The furnishings are old-fashioned. The colors are last century. And the grounds? Do not get me started."

"I rather like this room." I was surprised that His Highness sounded so pleasant. If I were a beast, I'd be tempted to bite her. Instead, he was looking around the great room as if he'd never seen it before.

"Don't be ridiculous," Juliette said derisively. "*None* of this will do. Surely you can see that."

"Some of this has importance for me," he said, staring at the half-finished painting above the mantle. It wasn't the subject matter he cared about, with its depiction of a very young and innocent version of the Prince. It was the painter who made that piece important. "I wouldn't be willing—"

"That's fine," Juliette interrupted. "We don't need to discuss it tonight. You'll see more clearly in the daylight, I'm sure."

"What I see is that you've had a long day," he said. "You should retire for the evening and we can talk again tomorrow."

Over the next few days, Juliette spent much of her time in the great room alone, marching about, muttering, "When this is MY castle, I'll change all this stodgy old stuff."

I didn't know how His Highness expected to fall in love with this girl. Robert kept reporting that His Highness was avoiding her. Probably because of her constant complaints. *I* would have avoided her, if I could.

The next evening, the two bumped into each other in the hall, once again forcing *me* to be an unwilling witness.

Juliette eyed His Highness critically. "Well, you look somewhat better today." That was true. His Highness must have spent hours trying to tame all that fur. She raised her eyebrows and demanded, "Do you love me yet?"

"Do I love you...?" The baffled expression on his face nearly made me laugh, but now was *not* the time to remind His Highness of my presence.

"No? Well, do not worry. I'm a very loveable person. I just hope you do so sooner rather than later. And hopefully before any kissing is involved. I think I must draw the line at kissing a Beast."

"Excuse me," His Highness bit out. "I have business to attend to." That cold, cutting tone was designed to put her in her place. It was sharp as a razor, but I thought most would not even realize they'd been cut until hours later.

"Go ahead," Juliette said, waving her hand around airily. "I'll just explore."

"You may go anywhere in the castle except the East Wing." This was uttered as an edict. An incontrovertible decree. "Heed me. No one may enter the East Wing!"

"Fine," Juliette said agreeably, though her pretty, little smile slid away. "Good day, then." I was immediately reminded that she was also part of the aristocracy. She might not be as skilled as His Highness, but she knew how to use that same cutting tone.

As soon as they left, I called out, "Moll?" Moll would have something insightful to say. Or if not insightful, then at least amusing. "Moll? Did you hear that?"

I waited, but her expected laugh did not come.

"Moll?" There was no answer, and I called out, desperation tingeing my voice as foreboding began to claw at my wooden frame. "Moll? Moll, dearest, please talk to me."

Again, silence was my only answer, and my sense of self wavered. Moll was my friend. She brought me moments of joy in this terrible half-life. If Moll was gone, I could almost wish the other books would fall silent as well.

Almost.

Only, the thought of continuing when all others were gone made my shelves sag. Could I be trapped here, alone, slowly fossilizing until, at the very last, nothing remained of me? Until what little of Lady Jayne Bea...Bea...Beatrice. Lady Jayne Beatrice Smythe would be gone as well?

Moll had made this existence tolerable. I already missed her sarcastic comments. Her glee at watching 'real life' stories play out in front of us. She would have loved the drama unfolding between Juliette and the Beast, and I missed…

I missed her.

"What is the point of continuing with no one left to care for?" I cried. Loneliness threatened to suffocate me; I wasn't sure I wanted to go on. Friendless. Alone once more.

Did I have a choice? And if I did, would I have the courage to do anything about it?

My voice emerged quite without my intention, nearly as wooden as my shelves. "I don't think I can bear being here alone."

I hadn't realized anyone else was there until the low voice spoke beside me. "I'm here, Lady Jayne." Robert offered those words hesitantly, as if not sure how I would take them. But he needn't have worried. My frame settled back against the wall and my shelves settled into place. Moll might be gone, but I wasn't alone.

The commotion began several hours later.

Yelling. Screeching. Bellowing.

Everyone in the castle must have heard it.

Robert swished in. "Lady Jayne, you are fortunate to be located here."

"Why would you say that?" I demanded. "You know how much I hate being stuck in this hallway."

"She went into the East Wing. The one we had to close off when the sparkles filled it up."

The East Wing? That foolish girl had ignored His Highness and gone into the East Wing?

Robert demanded, "Are you listening?"

"I...yes. Yes, I'm listening."

"That girl opened the door to the East Wing and now the entire hallway is blocked. Even worse, more of those shiny bits keep spilling into *our* wing. Who knows how far they'll reach—"

We both fell silent as footsteps pounded toward us. Robert leaned against the wall, then let himself slump against my side. That was the first time he'd ever touched me. I rather liked it.

Juliette hurried past me, stamping her feet with every step, leaving billows of pink and gold sparkles in her wake. Though I tried to suppress it, I sneezed as some settled onto my shelves. Fortunately, she didn't notice, but His Highness did. He shot me an admonishing look as he trailed after Juliette.

I nearly choked at the sight he made. His fur stuck out every which way, and every square inch was covered in sparkles. There were sparkles in his ears and stuck in his mane. His paws were obscured by sparkles up to his elbows.

He glittered more than the faceted glass chandelier hanging overhead.

Juliette snorted and coughed, deep racking coughs, and more sparkles shot out her nose as she sneezed. Far more loudly than I had; I knew how to sneeze like a lady.

She whirled on His Highness. "This is all your fault!"

"My fault?" Somehow, he managed to keep his voice calm and measured. "I told you not to go in the East Wing."

"I assumed there was something special that you were hiding beyond that door. Maybe you were hiding furnishings that would actually look acceptable in here."

"How did you manage to open it?" His Highness was finally losing his calm. I wouldn't want him staring at me like that. He looked fierce at all times, but when his lips pulled back off his teeth like that? He resembled one of the gargoyles of Notre Dame. "I keep that door locked."

Juliette didn't seem nervous as any rational person would be. "I know how to open a simple lock," she stated, nose in the air. "After wanting to read the diaries of eleven sisters who refused to tell me anything important, I taught myself."

"And you thought you'd use the skills of a thief in my castle?" His voice had dropped to what I thought of as his warning tone. His 'don't push me any further' tone. A bit silky. Deep and quietly menacing. I would have been quaking in my boots. If I had any. His eyes narrowed as he continued, "You had no right—"

"I wanted to see all of my castle!" she interrupted. She didn't seem to understand her peril.

The growl he uttered must have hurt his throat. It hurt mine to hear it. "This isn't your castle. It's *my* castle."

"Then why don't you act like it?" She gestured grandly at the sparkling mess around them. "How can you allow this to happen?"

Uh-oh. His roar shook the books on my shelves, making them dance in place. "This. Is. Not. My. Fault."

Juliette opened her mouth, but he didn't let her interrupt. He raised his voice in a bellow that made Robert tremble against me. "It's that wicked fairy. The one who cursed us. Blame her, not me. We had to shut that wing years ago." He roared again. Roared like a beast.

"Why would you shut up an entire wing of your castle?" Juliette seemed more appalled by that then any of his roaring. "That makes no sense!"

He was panting with irritation as she forced him to remember what none of us could endure to think about. "One of the servants disappeared in the East Wing years ago, when she was trying to clean out the sparkles," he bit out. "They kept increasing in there. Piling up, clogging the hallways."

One of the servants. He meant Rouge. Rouge had gone into the East Wing many years ago and never returned. We had never been particularly close, but we'd enjoyed each other's company. Back in the days when we were human she'd been Queen Marie's personal maid, and we'd often spent time together. For reasons known only to that horrible fairy, Rouge became a black tea towel when we were changed. Many, such as I, were unable to move about, so it fell upon others, like Rouge, to do the work of maintaining the castle. She'd gone to the East Wing years ago to dust and was never seen again.

The thought of being buried alive in glitter made me shudder hard enough that my every right angle creaked.

His Highness raked his claws through his mane. "We sent in search parties after her. The first two couldn't get through. The second group, some of my favorite servants, said they were barely able to fight their way back out. I should have paid attention. I should have given up. Instead, I sent in a third search party, determined to keep what belonged to me." He glared down at her, voice filled with bitterness. "I'd already lost so much. I couldn't bear to shut up an entire wing of my castle." His shoulders slumped, and he briefly closed his eyes. "That last group never returned. The stable boys, the steward, my favorite knights. They're lost, all of them, and presumed dead."

I had no idea he felt so badly about those that had been lost. If you'd asked me before, I would have said he cared nothing for any of his servants.

He gave a mighty shake, as if to dislodge that thought. I don't know if it helped clear his mind, but it did dislodge thousands of the glittering bits. Juliette shot His Highness a disgusted look. "You should call some of your seemingly non-existent servants to come and *groom* you."

Sparkles rose into the air and swirled about before dropping in untidy piles onto the floor. Unfortunately, many were still stuck all over the Beast's fur. So many it would take hours, and a great deal of painful effort, to get them all out.

Juliette glared at the mess, then turned and flounced from the room, more sparkles falling from her clothes with every step. Robert gave a low moan at the sight.

The strangled sounds leaking from the throat of His Highness made me worry that he was about to choke. Or worse, that he would manage to get the words stuck in his throat out and scare the foolish girl away. After all, she was probably just upset at nearly being trapped by pink and gold glitter.

No doubt she'd be better with some time to relax.

I was sadly mistaken.

Juliette swept into the great room the next morning, interrupting a pleasant talk I was having with Robert. He barely had time to slump against my side before she burst in muttering, "I refuse to wait. I'll turn this castle into a showplace, no matter what that wretched beast says."

She wrenched the painting off the wall with a muffled cry of triumph and stumbled back under its weight.

If you didn't know the story behind it, you might think the painting didn't belong in that room. Queen Marie had been working on it with Rebecca Tempera's assistance. It was a labor of love, up until she grew too ill to continue. I remembered the cry of satisfaction His Highness gave when he found it where his father had shoved it in a dark and dusty corner of the study, only a few years before the curse was cast.

His Highness had actually seemed content for a short time after finding it. He had placed it over the mantle with great reverence, and the painting had been in my line of sight ever since. I often wondered what it would have looked like if Queen Marie had been able to finish it.

Juliette staggered from the room. I heard her throw open a door, followed by a series of bangs and thumps as something (the painting, I presumed) tumbled down the stairs into the basement. A moment later, she marched back into the great room. I watched in horror, unable to do anything to stop her, as she tore the gold brocade curtains down from the windows. They ripped as she pulled and cursed at them, coming apart in several pieces.

Thank goodness none of the servants had been changed into curtains. But what if she decided to attack my books next? Or to re-upholster Theodore?

Quillsby took that moment to enter the hall to watch to spectacle. He perched on top of me, an itchy and annoying presence. I would have asked him to move, but just then Juliette stopped, placed her fists on her hips, and looked around the desecrated room, a smile of satisfaction playing on her lips.

I heard His Highness coming, even though it appeared that Juliette did not. When he entered that violated space, he stopped, momentarily frozen, then threw back his head and howled like a wounded animal.

Juliette narrowed her eyes at him, then pouted and fluttered those lashes again. "They were *hideous*."

"Now they're ruined," he growled.

"I did you a favor," she insisted, unrepentant. "You can never put those horrible things back up now. You'll have to get new ones."

"New—" He stopped dead, staring at the empty wall over the mantle. "Where is the painting?"

I had forgotten just how frightening the Beast could be. He was practically foaming at the mouth, rage barely contained.

"That thing?" Juliette sounded disdainful now. "I couldn't leave something like that in my gathering room where my guests could see it. It's a shame. The painting might have been nice if the artist hadn't been too lazy to bother finishing it."

"Lazy? Lazy?" He growled deep in his throat. "Where is it?"

Oh dear, his voice was nearly inaudible. Dangerously quiet. He reminded me of a great cat watching a mouse, preparing to leap upon it.

"I threw it in the basement," she said. That was far worse than how his father had ever treated the painting. Juliette finally seemed to realize her error. Her eyes widened as she took in the rage contorting his face. He was, at last, the epitome of a frighteningly hideous Beast.

I realized I hadn't seen him like this for many years now, so it was all the more shocking.

"You *threw* it in the *basement*." His words were filled with barely repressed violence. I was impressed that Juliette was able to remain standing there, rather than running in terror. It was enough to make me shake so hard the books jiggled on my shelves.

Juliette nodded slowly and hunched her shoulders as if to make herself smaller. For once there was no flirtatious smile. No pout or flutter of eyelashes. "Yes, I did, but I—"

The Beast drew himself to an imposing height; stretching up and out until the gold buttons on his dark green coat gave with a series of popping sounds, curved horns gleaming in the sun streaming through the uncovered windows. His eyes bulged as he thundered, "Enough! How would you like to be thrown into the basement?"

"N...n...n..." She stuttered.

"I expect you to pick up those curtains, repair them, wash them, and rehang them. *After* you put the painting back."

Juliette goggled, then spluttered, "You expect... Me? Wash them? Sew? Who do you... Uh! I certainly will not."

"You will." His Highness could have frozen a raging river with that voice. But it was his paws, curling and uncurling, each claw extended as far as it could go that held my attention. He hadn't let his claws show like that in decades. Not since he'd destroyed half of the South Wing in a fit of frustration.

What would become of me if he destroyed this part of the castle?

"I came here to save you from your curse," Juliette said haughtily. "But now I see you deserve it. That you could think a Beast — a Beast! — has the right to question me like this, after everything I've put up with. I... I..." She swung around, grabbed a large vase off the end table and threw it straight at his head.

His Highness had excellent reflexes in his beastly form. He ducked out of the way with no trouble and the vase shattered against the wall, adding even more mess to the ruined room. Next to me, Robert made a sound like a stifled sob.

The Beast looked at the shards of hand-painted glass. "What if that vase had been alive?"

I had expected him to be angry at the destruction of more of his possessions. I was surprised that his first thought was of us servants.

That surprised Juliette too. "You're crazy!" she shrieked. "It's just a vase. And an ugly one at that."

He gave a bark of laughter. "Did you really think I was here all alone? Look around. You are surrounded by my faithful servants."

"I will not stay here with a crazy beast," she shouted, red-faced and shaking. Though whether it was from fear or anger, I couldn't tell.

Juliette grabbed her rose-pink skirts in both hands, stepped over the torn curtains lying in forlorn heaps on the glitter-strewn parquet, and stalked to the front door. "Nothing is worth this," she shouted. Then she muttered, "I might enjoy being married to a wealthy merchant. I'll make him dress me better than any of my sisters. They'll all be jealous of my wardrobe. And my jewelry. I'll be the prettiest of them all!"

"You are just like my father, only interested in status and position. But I see what's important now. You are only pretty on the outside," His Highness yelled after her. "On the inside, you're about as appealing as…as…moldy bread!"

Well, so much for True Love.

# Chapter Eight:
## This Can't Continue!

In which a mop attempts to sweep away serious concerns

The argument had already raged for close to an hour. I knew many of my fellow servants were angry about being stuck as these confining objects after all this time. I would never be comfortable as the long, skinny mop I had been using when the curse hit. Why hadn't I been dusting the gallant, if somewhat stiff, suit of armor instead of Darwin? But even though I understood their frustration, I was surprised by the level of rage some were expressing.

"If the Beast can't control himself," Quillsby said ominously as he fluttered onto Theodore's high back, "we'll have to take control for him!"

I started to speak, "I really think—" But no one paid me the slightest attention.

"It was clearly the Beast's fault," Charles stated loudly, his strings vibrating with the force of his displeasure.

"That's not really fair," Theodore said reproachfully. He shuffled forward on his four stiff legs, nearly toppling Quillsby. "He did try. He's learning. But that girl pushed him too—"

"That girl was greatly misinformed on what a masterpiece looks like," Rebecca called from the music room. "How dare she throw Queen Marie's painting in the cellar." I wondered briefly what colors would be showing on her canvas.

"Rebecca, I haven't seen you in ages," Archambault said. He'd turned so fast at the sound of her voice that his feathered hat, tattered with age, nearly fell from where it hung at the top of his tall coat rack body.

"Well, you could come and visit those of us back here once in a while," Rebecca responded, but there was no reproach in her tone.

All of us who could move easily had managed to jam ourselves into the front hallway to discuss this latest debacle, while the others listened from the rooms where they were trapped. The Beast had locked himself in his rooms on the second floor, so everyone felt free to share their feelings without the slightest constraint.

Perhaps a bit of constraint would have made things more productive.

Many blamed the Beast for the angry departure of the girl. I understood their disappointment; I was just as tired of being a mop as the rest were of being coat racks and easels and chairs.

Well, perhaps not as much as some. I rather enjoyed my opportunities to speak to Lady Jayne. In her human form, she had been far above my station. She and I would likely never have spoken at all. But as a bookcase and a mop, matters of station didn't seem so important. I would miss our talks when we were Robert the Footman and Lady Jayne the Secretary once again. If that ever happened.

"You can't blame the Beast for the disastrous outcome with that girl," I said. And this time I managed to make myself heard.

Quillsby fluttered in anger where he still perched on Theodore's back. "I most certainly can! He—"

I interrupted quickly, "You were there, Quillsby. You saw what happened. The Beast acted with considerable restraint."

Behind me, someone yelled, "It has been three times already. How long do we have to—"

Whatever else they might have said was drowned out as Charles drew his bow across his strings in a shrieking dissonance. "Restraint?" he bellowed. "He threw her out. How can you call that restraint?"

"You didn't see her destroy the curtains his mother had chosen," I chided. "You didn't hear her talk about throwing the portrait his mother painted in the basement. You didn't hear her disparage everything he cared about. And you didn't hear how much he cares about us."

"None of that is an excuse," Quillsby stated imperiously. "Not when he knew how important she—"

"She refused to listen to him," Lady Jayne said sharply. "She's lucky he went into the East Wing after her. He could have just left her in there, lost forever like Rouge and the others."

There was a moment of complete silence. Rather like everyone in the room was holding their breath. No one was prepared to talk about those we had lost.

I scrubbed my way between the others until I was at the center of the angry mob. It was one of the advantages of being a slender object. I shook my mop strings with enough vigor that some of the others took a step back. "Besides," I said quickly, determined to keep this discussion on the important facts, "he didn't *throw* her out. She chose to leave. It's not like he could chase her down and drag her back."

"Oh, really?" Quillsby demanded. "That sounds just like something he would do."

"Don't be ridiculous," Theodore said, impatiently bouncing on his front legs and nearly knocking Quillsby off in the process. "Do you really think she'd ever fall in love with a Beast who refused to let her leave? That makes no sense, Quillsby." He finished this pronouncement with a derisive snort.

Darwin bit out, "Well, she'd have learned to forgive him. Someday."

Quillsby positively quivered with indignation, the feather on his quill fluttering wildly. "She'd see how desperate he is; how we *all* are. Anyone should understand that."

"No woman in her right mind would fall in True Love under those circumstances," Lady Jayne offered primly.

I edged a little closer to her, grateful for her calm, gentle support.

"He shouldn't have acted so...beastly," Quillsby insisted. "Then she wouldn't have left. We all know the truth. The Beast is out of control."

"Yes! The Beast is out of control and something must be done."

I twisted around, trying to see who had said that, but couldn't tell. "What exactly are you suggesting?"

For a moment no one answered, then a timid voice whispered, "Ahem. I think someone needs to speak to him about his temper." Archambault ducked behind Theodore when all eyes turned to him. As if his bright pink coat wasn't still clearly visible. He added mournfully, "It is better than it used to be, but it's still not good. He does need to control it, or we'll be stuck like this forever."

"He loves books," Hugo called from his painting in the library. "A pleasant surprise, I must admit. But what he needs is to read some good old-fashioned romances. South wall, shelves 19 through 22. They can inform him of the best ways to sweep a young lady off her feet."

Unbidden, a thought leapt into my mind. Maybe if I were a broom instead of a mop, I'd be able to sweep Lady Jayne off her feet… I quickly shook myself back to the matter at hand. "It has to happen soon," I said. "The sparkles are multiplying and may someday grow beyond my control. What happens to us if the entire castle fills with them?"

Arguments broke out all around me, punctuated by shouts and rising voices. I couldn't make out what everyone was saying, though that wasn't truly necessary. Their anger and frustration were palpable.

Then, in a strange break in the wall of sound, Darwin's voice rang out clearly from deep within the suit of armor. "The Beast had better fall in love with the next girl who walks through that door. Or else!"

Or else what?

# Chapter Nine:

## Beau

In which a fourth visitor causes a loyal armchair great
consternation

I t was winter again.

When I had been human—Theodore Bartleby,
butler for his Highness—I had loved the snow. It had
been a respite to my duties, an escape to remembered
childhood when I traipsed through the gardens. Now, as a
large armchair, the snow terrified me.

I had lost track of the years at this point, time turning
around its cosmic dance bringing the snow, the rain, the sun,
then snow again, all the sunrises and sunsets through the
windows of the castle that had blurred into this unchanging
now. Perhaps it had been almost eighty years we had lived
this half-life; I was not sure.

Always the Beast, pacing the halls, always the servants,
keeping the castle as clean as they could, what with the ever-
increasing glitter that accumulated in the corners. Our
routine had rubbed trails in the polished floorboards. His
paws, my wooden legs, as I followed him around.

"This is hopeless," the Beast lamented, collapsing onto
my threadbare cushions. I remembered when the fabric of
this armchair was bright and bold, a floral design in deep
crimson and sunny yellow. But the years of wear and layers
of fur had left my transformed hide a dingy brown.

But still I hoped I brought the Beast comfort.

"It is not hopeless as long as we have the means to feel hope," I attempted.

If there was anything these years had taught me, it was to no longer fear the wrath of the Beast. There was nothing he could do to us now, that the curse of that wretched fairy hadn't done worse.

At least, as the decades turned our struggle to capitulation, the Beast's anger had finally cooled.

"Quite a daring statement from a piece of furniture," he sighed, smoothing down the fur of his cheek. "But do we still feel hope? Do you?"

"Yes," I said immediately, as he leaned onto my other arm and crossed his legs.

His tail rapped against my side. "I wouldn't feel like this if I knew when another girl would wander my way… it's maddening, having no control! Being trapped!"

As I was formulating a rebuttal, Archambault stumbled in. His hat and fur coat, a bit worse for wear, were still draped from the upper hooks of his coat rack form.

"There's someone running up the lane!"

The Beast stood so swiftly that I skidded back across the wooden floorboards until toppling onto my back. I was so stunned, I almost missed the next exchange.

"Is this someone a girl?"

The coat rack audibly shuddered with a clacking of wood. "No, a young man—"

A roar escaped the Beast as what was surely a great surge of elation crashed into disappointment. "Turn him away."

"But, sir—"

"What?" the Beast challenged, facing him with hackles raised, his golden-brown hair sticking out enough to make his already-formidable form even larger.

Archambault's hat wobbled. "Sir, he's hurt."

"How does that concern me?"

My feet scraped the floor as I stood. "Because helping him would be the kind thing to do?"

The Beast growled, but did not turn to me. "We can't do that. I'll turn him away myself."

And off he stormed, Archambault and I scrambling after. I was just in time to hear the echo of the knocker, to see him throw open the large double doors. Flurries of snow and a blast of cold air wafted into the foyer, along with a hunched, snow-covered form that collapsed through the doors.

The Beast rolled him over roughly enough to suggest he planned to immediately throw him back into the cold. But then he paused, and his shoulders, and tail, lowered.

Archambault leaned over the Beast's shoulder. "My goodness. Are you truly going to turn him away?"

The Beast shook his head. "No, no. This is terrible. I can't send him back out like this. I *shouldn't*. We will help him."

I craned to see what state the man was in, but the Beast blocked my view. Above us came the sound of servants rustling on the upper floor of the foyer, most likely also trying to see.

The Beast's horned head twisted their way. "Don't just stand there, servants, I said help! Go prepare the first bedroom of the West Wing."

"But your highness, shouldn't he not see us—"

"The damn curse doesn't matter. With a wound like this he could die. He needs help. Now."

"I'll get cloth and warm water from the cooks," Darwin said, stomping off.

The Beast regarded the coat rack. "Archambault, get him a blanket."

And off he went.

Then the Beast turned toward me. "Theodore, come to me."

Shuffling closer, I finally got a glimpse of the young man who was now in the Beast's possession. The Beast had removed his damp cloak, and the man leaned on the Beast's arm, pale and trembling. He would have been quite handsome, blonde hair sweeping his forehead, and a fine stature, if it weren't for the source of alarm: a deep, bleeding gash from above his left eyebrow, across the bridge of his nose, and down his right cheek. The gash and the side of his face were caked in dirt and blood, as though perhaps he had fallen during his travels through the woods.

"Bring him upstairs to his room," the Beast told me, propping the man up in my chair, and then he pounded off toward the kitchens.

I stepped toward the grand staircase, trying valiantly to keep my traveler stable between my fabric arms; every jostle caused a groan to escape from him. Finally, I made it. By the time I squeezed through the door frame, the Beast had returned with Darwin, who had an armful of cloths and a pitcher of water. He took the man from my cushions and laid him in the bed, and to my surprise, the Beast—with his wide, furred shoulders, poufy mane, large upsweeping horns, his muzzle shaped in a snarl—picked up a dampened cloth and gently tended the man's wounds.

Then I realized, in the excitement, practically every servant in the house who could move had arrived to watch. And, of course, whisper.

"Who is he?"

"The Beast is actually helping him!"

"Perhaps the Beast has learned kindness?"

"But why this man?"

"Well, it's been so very long since our last visitor—"

"He's wasting his time. We need to be ready for a girl to come break the curse!"

And on they went, while the Beast tenderly worked, cleaning the blood and dirt from the man's face.

"He has a fever," the Beast whispered, and soon one of the servants put a damp cloth on his cleaned forehead.

"He needs ointment for the wound…" the Beast said next, and Archambault scampered off down the hall, returning swiftly with a bottle clasped between two wooden prongs. The Beast took it from him and readied a cloth.

Then he steeled himself and poured the ointment into the gash on the man's face.

For the first time since arriving, the man moved—his eyes flew open and he screamed. The servants recoiled, but the Beast ignored the sound and pressed the cloth into the gash, his other hand pushing firmly on the man's chest to keep him in place.

When the man's cries stopped, the Beast sat back. The alarm was inescapable on the man's face, and who could blame him? He was surrounded by nightmares—a terrific demon and furniture with eyes. But he had stopped shouting, and instead stared at us all in turn, with pale green eyes that shone with fascination and horror. Finally, his gaze landed on the Beast. He breathed deeply as he scanned the Beast's formidable stature.

"I am dead then," the man rasped. "For you are the devil, here to punish me for my sins."

The Beast shook his head. "You are not dead."

The man blinked, scanning the servants around him. "Then what magic is this?"

"A horrible curse from an even more horrible fairy."

"Who are you?"

"Just a Beast, now," the Beast said, sitting up with back straight, towering over the bed. "And who are you?"

"My name is Beau," the man said, then his eyes fluttered and he groaned.

"You will rest here tonight," the Beast said.

But the man was already asleep.

The Beast let out a heaving sigh. "Leave us, all of you. Please."

And as we obeyed, the whispers started back up again. What had we just witnessed? And what would it mean for the Beast, and the curse?

Several days passed before our visitor was strong enough to leave his bed, and during much of that time the Beast had been there, tending to him. Keeping his wound cleaned and medicated, bringing him food and drink. And in the later days, they talked. Many of us listened in from the hallway, surprised not only at our continued visitor but in the demeanor of both him and the Beast.

But there were things neither of them wanted to talk about – whenever the Beast asked Beau how he got hurt, he would turn his head and gaze out the window. And whenever Beau would ask who the Beast was before the curse, the Beast would growl and sulk.

And so it went, until our visitor became strong enough to stand. Then the Beast decided to show him around the castle, and all of us frenzied to clean the place as well we could, what with the eddies of sparkles that had collected since we all had become transfixed with Beau.

I helped the Beast pick out one of the more vibrant red robes that had been modified to fit his new form, gold-flecked trim bringing out the rich brown hues of his fur. As we went to fetch Beau, we passed Robert. He was pushing mounds of sparkles toward the East Wing, now filled to its limit, the sparkles in heaps that nearly blocked the door from view.

When the Beast and Beau exited the West Wing, they could see across the foyer to Robert as he worked.

"So that's why you're full of glitter," Beau laughed at the Beast.

"It doesn't come off," the Beast growled.

"Give me a coarse brush and some powder and I'll get you cleaned up," Beau announced.

The Beast blinked, his chest rising with a deep breath.

Beau smiled. "It is the least I could do for your kindness."

And perhaps I was imagining a lightness in the Beast's steps, as they continued their slow tour through the castle. Beau had to stop frequently to rest, and soon the Beast had me follow him around, ready to give him a seat when he needed.

"I am so sorry to sit on you," he said, every time.

"No need to apologize to someone who is doing their job," I replied.

In the grand foyer, Beau gazed up at the curtains, torn down by that selfish girl and carefully hung again, and Queen Marie's unfinished painting, salvaged and rehung despite the new gash it had across the Beast's princely face, from falling down the stairs.

"What happened here?" he asked softly.

"Not everyone appreciates when sentimentality overrides aesthetics," the Beast carefully explained. "Someone I care about greatly picked out those curtains and painted that painting. I want to keep them on display."

"That you should. The fabric is lovely. It's a shame about the rip in the painting, though."

The Beast shrugged. "I don't think it detracts from being able to admire the piece."

Beau brought a hand up to the dark scabs on his own face, and smiled. Soon, they moved on.

Everywhere the Beast and Beau went, they spoke gently, the Beast introducing each servant and telling him of them before the curse had befallen. At first I had been amazed the Beast had paid so much attention before the curse, until I realized, no, he had listened to us after. In the years of our solitude, he had listened to the stories we had told, all we had left of ourselves, and he had remembered.

Soon, our visitor gained enough strength to walk about the castle with ease. But somehow the topic of him leaving never came up. It perplexed many servants, and whispers of despair had started. One evening, many of us happened to cross paths in the hall foyer.

The inevitable topic of the Beast and Beau came up.

"He no longer cares to end the curse," Lady Jayne cried, her books fluttering on their shelves.

"Where are they now?" Darwin asked, his armor creaking, and then of course they turned to me.

"They're in the master's study by the fire," I said.

"What are they doing?" Robert demanded, hopping on his mop-head.

"Talking, last time I checked."

"But why, why is he wasting his time?" Robert asked, leaning against Lady Jayne with a sigh.

"I don't know," I told others, but truth be told, deep inside me, I did know.

I just didn't know what it would mean, if I were right.

As Beau's wound healed to a thick pink line that bisected his face, he and the Beast began to spend much time in the library. I was with them, as they happened past the modern history books, and Beau took out a tome. He leaned against a bookshelf and began to read aloud, but when the name of the kingdom and the Beast's family passed his lips, the Beast roared and smacked the book from his hands.

Beau stood stunned, fear lining his wide eyes, as the Beast snarled at the discarded book. Isadora had cautiously swung over to see what was happening, Hugo leaned precariously out of his frame, and time hung frozen for several moments as we waited to see what would happen next.

"What did I do wrong?" Beau said, his voice light.

The Beast turned to him, his teeth still bared and his hackles still raised, snorting roughly through his nose. I trembled on my little wooden legs, inwardly begging the Beast to stay good and kind and, most of all, forgiving.

Finally, slowly, the Beast's snorting calmed, and Beau's eyes relaxed.

"You . . . you did nothing wrong." The Beast sighed, his tail twitching slowly, as he picked up the tome, and turned a few pages.

"Is that book about your family?" Beau asked, taking a step toward the Beast.

"Yes. Here is the castle where we are now, before the woods and curse began to swallow it whole." He then turned another page. "And here are my mother and father."

Beau looked on, and reached out a hand to touch the Beast's shoulder. There was a flinch and a snarl, but then their eyes met again and the Beast calmed, released a breath, and returned his attention to the book.

"What happened?" Beau asked cautiously. In the air hung an unspoken understanding that he meant the curse, the Beast's form, that moment when everything changed.

"I cannot tell you yet."

"Can you yet tell me your name?" Beau asked, the heaviness of his regard enough for the Beast to pause at great length.

I realized then that as the years had gone on, we had almost forgotten the Prince that was, consumed by the image and disposition of the Beast instead. What he had been before the curse led to that singular moment of irreverence and pride, but then the resulting Beastliness became all-encompassing. As I watched the two men, I could hardly recall the Beast's given name myself.

Finally, the Beast spoke. "My name is Estienne."

And when Beau smiled at him, it took my breath away. It was only later, recalling that moment, I realized that what had truly squeezed my heart . . . was hope.

My hopeful sentiment was not shared amongst the others. Isadora and Hugo had shared their versions of the Beast and Beau's exchange with Quillsby, and thanks to him, rumors literally flew rampant through the castle.

"I heard the Beast tell that man how much he loves being a beast," Quillsby proclaimed, floating about the study around Maximus, while Rebecca and Charles looked on.

"He couldn't possibly, how monstrous," Rebecca fretted, as Maximus played a discordant tune. His voice had all but left him as of late.

"It would be like one of us saying we love these bodies," Charles said, echoing with frustration within his wooden form.

"Impossible," Rebecca remarked, as a purple-hued illustration of a flower-filled valley bathed in moonlight spread across her canvas. Maximus agreed with Charles' sentiment with well-timed strong chords, but due to the years and the sparkles, there were gaps in his tune.

"I remain desperate to turn back," Quillsby muttered.

"It's been so long; will we know what to do with ourselves as humans again?" I asked, and the instruments and easel turned to me. We rarely talked pointedly about the time that had passed, especially as the years had become decades. We had spent an entire human lifetime like this. I wasn't sure I could remember the taste of food. Or even how to walk with two legs.

"Well, . . . of course we will," Rebecca replied, but the hesitance and softness of her voice, and the way her canvas turned a muddled gray, only helped to prove my point.

Quillsby flipped around in the air. "We have to help the Beast end this curse. Before we are all lost."

"Before the sparkles from the curse take over," Charles said.

I took notice then of the heaps of sparkles glittering in the corners of the study. We hadn't been as diligent with cleaning them since our visitor had arrived. Or were they possibly accumulating more quickly? It was an unsettling feeling, to have what had brought me so much hope, plunge into fear instead.

The others continued to theorize about the Beast no longer caring for his future or the future of his servants, as though the act of him befriending someone somehow meant he would always remain a beast.

And I creaked in place, no longer sure what to believe.

One early morning, the Beast built a fire in the study as rain began to fall. It was the first sign of spring we had witnessed, an apparent warming of the winds to bring rain instead of snow.

The Beast reclined on my upholstery now, gazing out the study's window as Beau sat on a chair beside him, tea in hand.

"Does spring ever make you sad?" Beau asked, and the Beast tilted his head at him, the gesture even more grand thanks to his horns.

"Why would it do that? With the new growth and flowers and warm air?"

"Exactly that," Beau lamented, sipping his tea and letting out a sigh. "Spring brings with it such expectations, of fair-weather parties and trite conversations and all the burdens of socializing in a world that doesn't feel right."

"I was not the man who would have noticed those things," the Beast admitted. "Not before this." He gestured at his body.

Beau sat straighter in his chair. "What would you have noticed?"

"I was the one demanding perfection and orchestrating the conversations," the Beast said. "I was the one punishing the mistakes and shunning the non-conformers."

"Is that how you came to be cursed?" Beau asked hesitantly.

"My selfishness cursed me. My pride and my foolishness. And it cursed not just me but everyone who had ever been around to support me. My failure became their burden to bear too."

To hear him say it, so clearly, so heartfelt, I had never truly expected. But there it was.

"Somehow my failure became my family's to bear as well," Beau said. "But please, my troubles are little compared to yours."

"No trouble is little if it is affecting your life to that point," the Beast challenged, gesturing at Beau's face.

Beau cleared his throat, and put down his teacup. "My father would not call it little either. A man is supposed to bring his family a pretty young woman to make his wife. And with that marriage, the sons to continue the family legacy. No wife means no sons, means no future, means no family support."

The Beast had perched at the end of my cushion, leaning forward as the man talked. "You could not find a girl?" he asked, the curiosity in his tone revealing his excitement.

Beau shook his head. "It did not take courting many girls for me to realize my life was not taking me down that path."

"So, your family shunned you because you could not choose? Why, our problems are one and the same. I remain cursed because I cannot find a girl to love, who will love me in return."

"No, dear Beast," Beau whispered, and I stifled my surprise as well as I could when he reached forward, running a fingertip down the length of one of the Beast's horns. The Beast shuddered but did not recoil. "My family shunned me not because I could not choose, but because I would not. They cast me to the woods in the middle of that snowy night, where, with the threat of wolves in my wake, I ran and ran. In my fright, I tripped, and a tree branch tore open my face, mutilating me, branding me for the rest of my life—because I would never choose a girl."

The Beast shook his head slowly. "Beau . . . you are not mutilated."

"Estienne, do you understand my meaning?" Beau said in a strained voice, as his fingers drifted from the Beast's horn to his furred cheek.

Then, the Beast answered in a way I did not expect, that I had only dreamed was possible.

"And do you understand mine? You are possibly the most beautiful man I have ever known."

The Beast's confession and Beau's truth hung in the air, and, like the ever-steady fall of sparkles, they slowly settled onto the two men, and the servants who had been brave enough to sneak near. I tried desperately to remain still with the Beast upon me, to not let a single creak or twitch of cloth interrupt the magic that was transpiring before us.

Beau let out a soft gasp as the Beast laid his hand over Beau's. For a wonderful moment, the possibility of happiness shone.

"Perhaps it is fate that you came upon my castle."

But then Beau took his hand away, and with great sadness in his eyes, said, "All I could ever do is hurt you, if a girl must break your curse."

"The greater pain would be if you leave," the Beast countered.

"I've been foolish to stay so long. I have been hiding from my troubles, and helping you hide from yours." Beau stood, and the Beast rose immediately after, reaching a clawed hand to rest gently on his shoulder.

"Must you leave?"

Beau removed the Beast's hand and took two steps backward toward the door. "I want you to find humanity and happiness again."

The Beast clasped his hands tightly to his chest, and his voice wavered as he said, "I have felt more human these past weeks as a Beast in your presence than I ever did all those years ago as a Prince."

My heart wept at the Beast's words. But the look in Beau's eyes was only that of admiration, or perhaps longing.

"Thank you so much for your kindness, your hospitality. If only all men could be as you have been to me."

"Please, Beau, please don't go."

"It is because I care for you that I must."

And as he left, the Beast went after him, servants scuttling out of the way in the halls as they passed. I galloped to keep up, still too stunned by what had transpired to speak, to try to convince the young man to stay.

The Beast stopped in the foyer as Beau donned his cloak, pulled open the grand door, and disappeared into the gray, wet morning.

And the anguished howl that escaped the Beast will haunt me for the rest of my days.

The greatest despair had befallen the castle. As the hours passed, wailing winds and harsh rain pounded the castle walls, and the Beast lay consumed with grief, locked in his bedchambers at the end of the West Wing. But worst of all, the servants had all gone mad.

Many were certain we would never be human again, and worse, that the Beast would die and the fairy would return and somehow put blame on us. The duties that had become so important a routine for those of us who could move, that had become erratic when Beau arrived, completely ceased upon his departure. Navigating the halls and the grand staircase soon involved struggling against swaths of dazzling dust.

"We have to stop this," Quillsby proclaimed, his roughened feather quivering.

"And how do you propose we do that?" I asked.

"We give the Beast an ultimatum," a voice boomed.

We turned to find Darwin at the top of the staircase, the joints of his armor so packed with sparkles that his movements were stiff.

"My good sir, what exactly do you have in mind?" Quillsby asked.

"He must break the curse or face our wrath."

"Preposterous," some of the servants cried. "Impossible."

Robert stood beside Darwin, his mop-head caked with sparkles. "We cannot be trapped here. It will not end like this. Not when we have so much we could live for, not when we have people we love." He glanced down the stairs, where Lady Jayne stood in the shadows.

Then Darwin picked Robert up, and held the mop out like a sword. "Who will go with me to challenge the Beast?"

"Don't do this," I said, but my voice was drowned out by the chorus of agreement, from the creaking of wood to the humming of strings. They shuffled, bounced and climbed up the stairs, and I followed behind with an ever-growing dread in my heart. Outside, the rain continued to pour, darkness and chill enveloping the castle.

There was no way this could end well.

The servants burst into the Beast's chambers, where the dark red curtains of his large bed were drawn tight. Out the bedroom windows, little light came in through the clouds. But a burst of lightning flashed sparkles that floated in the air, reflecting gleams of pink about the room.

"Go away," the Beast choked from behind the bed curtain.

"This must end today!" Darwin declared, throwing the curtain back, but the Beast hid under richly colored blankets. Darwin's declaration was followed by roars of agreement from the servants. "We will no longer wait for you to choose to end the curse! It is ending now!"

"How do you expect to do that?" the Beast's muffled growl came.

"Why did you waste so much time with Beau?" Archambault asked.

"You can't possibly want to stay a Beast," Charles strummed.

"You don't care about us!" Robert cried.

As the others added their voices to the cacophony, I stood behind them in horror, unwilling to raise my voice in an attempt to get them to stop.

Then finally, the Beast uttered a mighty roar, throwing the blankets from himself to reveal his tattered, glitter-filled fur and furious snarl. Another bolt of lightning highlighted his horrifying features.

"Enough!"

The uproar hushed as many servants leaned back, like the mere inches of distance they added between themselves and the Beast would be enough to save them from his wrath.

"You couldn't see how much I cared for him?" the Beast said, his fist clasped upon his chest. "I would change this if I could! I would love the next girl to cross through those doors, if I knew it wouldn't be a lie."

"A lie wouldn't end the curse," I said, and many eyes darted my way before refocusing on the Beast.

Rebecca's frame creaked. "But will your love for Beau, monsieur?"

Everyone's silence gave way to the pounding of the rain and howling wind, as the Beast stood on the bed and we all waited, breaths held, for what would happen next.

"No, I don't think it will. Perhaps I must remove myself from all of this."

"Your Highness?" Archambault said, his voice wavering.

"Perhaps, if I perish, the curse will end for all of you."

The Beast stood to his full height, and leapt off the bed, over us. He bounded down the hall, down the stairs, and we all stumbled over each other to follow, some of us shouting for him to go, others for him to stay, and in the confusion of it all, I would not be able to say who was on which side.

We tumbled down the stairs in his wake, the fall softened by the piles of sparkles on the steps.

"What if we die when you do?" I strained to ask, but in all the commotion, no one heard, and before we could stop him, the Beast disappeared into the storm.

The moment the Beast left the castle, we knew something was horribly wrong. The creak and whine of strained wood echoed through the halls and towers, which, accompanied by the force of the wind and rain, made us fear the entire castle coming down. Sparkles fell like snow, catching the candlelight like pink-gold stars twinkling.

It was the thickest and fastest the magic had ever been. Servants spoke over each other in a confused rush.

"We're sure to die."

"He's abandoned us."

"Why did we drive him away?"

"Theodore, we have to get out of here."

The last words caught my attention enough for me to look up from my despair. There was Archambault, repositioning his hat and helping Rebecca to her easel legs.

"Why?" I asked helplessly.

"The sparkles are growing," Archambault lamented, the layers of glitter becoming thicker on the floor even as we watched. Robert swept them into the corners, Quillsby flew about dusting little paths on the staircase banisters—

"If we stay here, I don't know what will become of us," Archambault continued.

"But what about the Beast?" I cried.

"What could we do?"

"We must get to higher ground, before the sparkles drown us," Darwin said, helping the others up the grand staircase, the steps now slippery with mounds of sparkles. But going up could mean being trapped. It could mean being swallowed whole by the castle and the suffocating sparkles. I was too terrified to go up, too terrified to go out, and instead stood in place, like the glitter had solidified around me.

And then the grand doors swung open, wind and rain pushing the piles of sparkles deeper into the foyer. There, in a drenched cloak, stood Beau.

"You have returned!" I cried.

"Where is he?" Beau asked. "I saw the storm gather above the castle from miles away. I knew something must be horribly wrong—I could not stay away."

"The Beast has abandoned us," Archambault managed, the wet wind throwing his hat from his hooks.

"Where would he go?"

When we did not respond, Beau repeated the question, the fear and concern in his voice shaking me to my core.

"We should know this!" This time the words came from Archambault, and they were directed at me.

"I don't know, why would we know?" I replied.

"We used to travel with him to the outside, before all this, do you remember?"

Even the words he used overwhelmed me. "No, no, I don't remember outside the castle—"

"We carried his effects and readied his carriages," Archambault continued, his voice wavering, like it pained him to remember the outside world. I tried to recall: the front path, the gardens to the left, the stable to the right, the bridge . . . over . . . the . . . what was it? I could hear the rushing sound, the bubbling something beyond the hedges—

"The river!"

My excitement at recalling things that far away quickly fell into peril. Beau's expression stretched thin.

"No. No, no, no. I will go to him, before it's too late," he declared, clutching his cloak to his chest with a tight fist.

Then off he ran, back into the storm, the doors still wide, water mixing with the glitter into a deadly soup.

"We need to help him." I couldn't believe these words had left me.

"Theodore, you must go, you are faster than me." Archambault waved his small arms, his coat rack legs hardly visible above the glitter.

"But it's raining, I would get soaked!" I cried. The storm punctuated my fear with another bright flash, a pink explosion of light. The rain, a torrent of wet, scared me to my core—my wooden, vulnerable core. If I spent too long in the downpour, would it ruin me?

"I will go with you."

It was Darwin, holding Robert still.

"No, *we* will go with you!" the mop added.

Darwin's formidable stature and Robert's immediate support gave me unexpected confidence.

"Together, we may be able to save him yet," I declared.

And when I galloped into the rain, Darwin's rusty joints screeched beside me.

It was far worse outside than I could have imagined. The rain beat down on us, and when I dared to look back, the castle was shrouded in clouds that flashed strangely pink. I shivered as I saw we left sparkles in our wake, swirling eerily into the slushy snow.

Ahead, I spotted Beau, his dark cloak streaming out behind him as he ran, his arm across his face to shield him. Past him, I could make out the large stone bridge that crossed the river. There was no sign of the Beast.

I pushed forward, the rain soaking into my fabric, into my wooden frame, weighing me down. Darwin seemed similarly hindered, as he held Robert aloft ahead of him. Forward we strode. And when we reached the bridge, Beau gasped and pointed down at the river.

There, the Beast floated with the current, the river bloated and swift due to the rain. Beau ran to the river's sandy bank downstream of him, calling the Beast's name into the wind.

Then the Beast's head raised out of the water. When he reached out a hand toward Beau, and began struggling against the current, my breath caught with relief. But I dared not go closer, the rain still slowing me, and the mud an even more formidable enemy.

But closer, Darwin went. He struggled to the bank, his joints stiffer than I had ever seen them.

I could just barely make out Robert's voice in the storm. "Point me toward him!"

With Beau's help, Darwin held Robert out, above the water, to hopefully intersect with the Beast as the current pushed him downstream.

The Beast reached for Robert, and his mop strings reached back. Then a surge in the current pulled the Beast under. With a yelp, Darwin lurched forward—I couldn't hear the splash as he too went under.

I feared the worst, my helplessness and despair insurmountable. Beau called the Beast's name and ran down the bank. For a terrible moment, with the rain still soaking me, nothing happened. Then it was with uncontainable elation that I cheered when Robert reemerged from the water, clasped tightly by Darwin, dragging the Beast by his cloak. They all collapsed onto the shore. Beau met them, and soon gestured up at me to join them.

With Darwin's help, the Beast was placed upon me, my damp upholstery stretching from the strain.

"He's alive," Beau said, his wide eyes shining. "But he's unconscious and shivering. We need to get him back inside."

We made a much slower trek back to the castle, in the wind and cold.

Finally, we passed through the castle's grand doors, and I slipped past piles of wet sparkles until we reached the closest fire. Servants gasped and cried and let us through. Once there, I dropped to the floor, my legs giving way underneath me.

Darwin graciously relieved me of my burden, laying the Beast close to the warm fire. Beau collapsed by his side.

"Estienne, I am here. I came back!" He shook the Beast's shoulders, and when the Beast remained still, Beau cried out, "I shouldn't have left you, I shouldn't have been afraid. Now I'm only afraid to lose you!"

"But you cannot break the curse," Archambault said, his voice heavy with remorse, while many of the others voiced their agreement.

"Did that evil fairy truly say that a woman had to break the curse?" Beau demanded. "I love him, I love my Beast— isn't that enough? Isn't that what matters?"

Rumbling surrounded us—an unsettling reverberation— that started quietly everywhere at once, then grew and grew. A peculiar feeling began within me; it spread out through my frame, then my batting and fabric. Around me, the other servants became restless, and their unrest grew with the noise that was rapidly increasing.

A wind picked up, taking with it swirls of sparkles. And as the wind increased in speed, the sparkles reflected an unknown light, and became so thick and bright in the air that

I was blinded. And that strange feeling within me grew in equal measure, until for an intense moment I was overwhelmed with feeling and sound and pink light.

When my vision returned, I blinked, and coughed, the sparkles caught in my throat.

My throat. My *throat*. My hands shot to my neck, my cheeks, and I took a deep breath and cried out in triumph. I was me again! Flesh and bone and blood and the same butler's coat and vest I had worn all those very many years ago. And I could recall the castle grounds, and the river and valley and villages beyond. I could recall Paris, and France, and the world. I wept, and the warm tears on my cheeks were the best blessing.

Finally, I could take in the sight before me, the other servants—my friends and colleagues, similarly transformed.

And in the center of it all, the Beast—no, Prince Estienne—sat up, his long brown hair in wet tangles across his cheeks. Beau brushed the hair out of his face, and the men laughed, a tender, beautiful sound.

Beau helped the Prince to his feet, helped him pull his now-oversized dress coat around his human shoulders. And as they clasped their hands together, I felt the joy of the lifted curse, the freedom of the people around me, crying and cheering and embracing each other in turn. There was Maximus, holding Rebecca tightly. There was Lady Jayne, her arms thrown around Robert. There was Archambault, adjusting the pink coat on his shoulders, a magnificent smile gracing his human features.

The cursed sparkles had all but vanished, their remnants glittering faintly in the air. The rain had let up, clouds parting enough for the sun to shine brightly through the windows. And there, in the sunlight, Beau and the Prince embraced.

"And to think, I had been looking forward to kissing a Beast," Beau laughed, and when the Prince bared his teeth in an alluring smile, Beau pulled him into a kiss.

We clapped and cheered, for the triumph of hope and love in all its forms.

# Chapter Ten:

## ...And They All Lived Happily Ever After

In which a certain person misses the point of it all

I was on my way to a royal christening (the only kind I attend, obviously) when magical senses mortals simply don't understand told me that something very, very strange was happening at a castle I'd cursed some decades before. I *never* shirked my responsibilities, so I flitted there at once to investigate.

Imagine my shock to arrive at a wet, slushy castle with not a single lovely sparkle in sight! By now the dreary place should have been very nicely ornamented.

I flew in the front door with a trail of pink and gold sparkles to find a scene of utter chaos in the front hall. Servants were running about everywhere, embracing each other in a perfectly absurd display. Why weren't they objects?

The only sparkles in sight were on a bedraggled group of stable boys and the like who had evidently just stumbled in, led by some little parlor maid. All of them were being greeted as though their existence was simply miraculous.

Why would anyone pay attention to a parlor maid when *I* was here?

The only one looking in my direction was a freckled footman in a fur coat as pink as my dress, with a lovely feathered hat, who was staring at me with enormous eyes.

"More sparkles," he murmured, backing up and bumping into a faded armchair. "Oh—sorry, Theodore." Then the footman blinked at the armchair. "Wait, you're not Theodore…"

"Definitely not," a nearby man in a brocaded waistcoat said with a grin not nearly formal enough for his coat.

How dare they pay attention to each other instead of to me? "Where," I demanded, "is the Beast?"

Now at last heads were turning toward me, and out of the middle of the tumult a tall, broad-shouldered man who looked vaguely familiar stepped forward. "I believe you mean me," he said with a wide smile.

Perhaps the smile was why I didn't recognize him at first. He had certainly not smiled before. Or perhaps because, after all, I saw so many, many princes. Or perhaps because this was all just *wrong*.

"Oh no, no, no, no, no, no!" I scolded. "You weren't supposed to break the curse yet. You were supposed to be enchanted for a good solid century, and it's been barely more than eighty years!"

"Perhaps," he said, glancing toward a scarred man beside him. "But I've found true love."

"I hardly think so," I scoffed. "I'm sure you're simply infatuated with a pretty face, and something has gone wrong with the magic. Say something rude to me, and I'll re-enchant you."

"I wouldn't mind," the scarred man murmured, with a rather provoking smile.

Meanwhile a gasp went up from the servants, who had previously fallen respectfully silent. I was glad to see *they* understood the gravity of the situation.

The Prince glanced around at the faces turning toward him with alarmed expressions, and still smiled. "Gracious lady, I would never dream of being so unchivalrous to you, or so inconsiderate of my companions in distress. I think we've all been cursed long enough."

A cheer went up around him, which I attempted to suppress with the stern reminder, "Servants are not companions. They are servants. And you don't even have to be *very* rude. I can be flexible."

"Besides," he continued, "I did find true love, just as you said. And I thank you for your help."

This gave me pause. Perhaps he had learned something after all. Few people grow enlightened enough to value the great service I do for them. Perhaps I would mercifully and graciously accept his claim to have properly found True Love after all.

Before I could speak further, a fussy man with fluffy white hair came strutting up, chest out importantly and quill pen waving in one hand, and announced, "I hardly think we ought to be thanking this terrible woman for her enchantment." He pointed the quill pen at me. "Do you realize, madam, that we nearly drowned in sparkles? If the curse had lasted a century, we would have all died! We believed until today that many of us *had* died," he concluded, jabbing his quill toward the bedraggled assortment of servants with sparkles in their hair.

I gave this impertinent man my frostiest stare. "If an entire castle of enchanted servants could not clean up a few sparkles, I hardly think I can be blamed for that."

He turned red. "A *few*—"

"And just who are you?" I demanded. "Are you some sort of nobility? Shall I curse the lot of you again for *your* rudeness?"

More gasps went up in the crowd, and the angry man snapped, "I am the castle scribe and—"

"Oh, another servant," I said with a wave of my hand. "Well, you're not important enough to deserve one of my educational and enlightening curses. Apologize at once and we'll say no more about it."

"Not important enough—" the man began, but then was seized on either side by the two men who had greeted me, who had been grinning so happily before.

"He's sorry," the one with the brocaded waistcoat said.

The one with the pink fur coat nodded vigorously. "Very sorry!"

And then they hustled him away. Quite right—as if I should be bothered with such nonsense.

"Now then, your highness," I said, firmly returning my attention to someone who mattered. "I *suppose* I will accept that you learned something worthwhile. Perhaps. Now show me this True Love of yours."

The Prince—what was his name? Oh yes, Estienne—beamed at me, and his eyes did have that True Love sparkle to them. I began to feel a bit more mollified—until he drew forward the scarred man. "My lady, this is Beau."

"I've heard so much about you," Beau remarked, and his eyes sparkled too.

I blinked. I blinked again. This…was not expected. "Oh. Oh, I see. Well. That's queer."

And they both had the audacity to grin at me. But, well—it did appear to be True Love. I sighed. "I *still* feel it would have been more proper to wait another twenty years for the lovely girl I am sure will be coming along. But it's hard to argue with True Love, after all."

"Yes, it is," Prince Estienne agreed, and then had the audacity to look away from me to the silly, milling servants. He singled out a rather dashing gentleman and the dark-haired woman clinging to his arm. "Maximus, Rebecca, I know you've been waiting for my permission to wed. I give it to you! I should have given it to you long before this curse ever came to us."

That seemed proper enough, one of the duties of royalty.

Maximus's eyes grew wide, while Rebecca leaned in closer to him with a bright smile and tears in her eyes. "Thank you, my Lord," Maximus murmured.

Rebecca turned towards him, framing his face with her hands. "We can still have what you promised, Maximus. If the offer is still valid, of course. We have waited so long to be together."

"And I never should have made you wait," Prince Estienne said, one arm still around the scarred man—Beau, that is. I'd have to look into his genealogy, see if he was really suitable.

Maximus bowed to the Prince, then turned to Rebecca. "My dearest, my heart beats but for you—now, dare I say it, may I escort you to your room?"

She smiled up at him and said, "You may." And they set off together out of the room that very moment.

I sniffed. "Well, *that* doesn't seem altogether proper. You'd think they could be more patient."

"True love should never be delayed," Prince Estienne said firmly, and turned to smile at Beau again.

"Commoners don't have True Love," I said in my best quelling tones.

But he was distracted, looking for someone else in the crowd. He was ignoring my wise advice! Perhaps he hadn't learned as much as I had hoped, if he could be so inconsiderate. I was tempted to leave at once, but my instinct for doing good told me there was still so much I could teach here.

Prince Estienne seemed to be interested in an older man standing by an open doorway into the library, eagerly perusing a green jacketed volume. "Hugo," the Prince called, "why don't you get your head out of your botany books and start courting Isadora? Hasn't she been waiting long enough too?"

Hugo looked up and blinked rapidly, darting glances at the blushing woman standing nearby. "Oh, I—I mean I never—that is, I didn't—well, now that you mention it—but how did you…"

"Oh come on, Hugo," Isadora said with a giggle, and pulled him through the doorway into the library.

"Perhaps you are getting a little *too involved*, your highness?" I hinted. "After all, they're *servants*."

"Who became my friends," he said without a trace of shame. "I am only sorry it took so long."

I was aghast.

"All these divisions get so ridiculous," Prince Estienne continued. "Isn't that the point? To look past what people seem to be on the outside to who they really are inside?"

"Oh no, no, no, that is *not* the point," I protested. "Not like *this*." And he still wasn't listening!

He was looking at yet *another* couple, a truly gracious woman with several books under one arm, standing beside a tall, thin footman with stringy hair. "Robert," Prince Estienne said, "I know you worry that you're not a high enough rank for Lady Jayne. Fine—I make you a lord. Problem solved!"

Lady Jayne laughed and Robert mumbled thanks and I had had *quite* enough of all this. You *cannot* just make someone a lord. There is a Proper Way to do things and this was decidedly not it.

"You," I said frostily to the Prince, "have clearly learned nothing."

And he *laughed*! And called to two musicians, "Charles, Victor, give us some music!" He turned to Beau and gave a slight bow. "May I have this dance?"

"Always," Beau said with a rakish grin, and they swept off together as a violinist and a cellist struck up a jaunty tune.

The servants started dancing too, some in pairs, some in great swinging circles. Several women in kitchen uniforms entered the hall carrying great platters of bread and cheese and possibly a fondue pot. And *no one* was paying attention to *me!*

I was sorely tempted to curse them again after all, just for impertinence. But...he did thank me. And he did find True Love.

I put my hands on my hips and announced, "I never stay where I am not appreciated. None of you deserve me!" And I vanished, shooting a shower of sparkles over the crowd.

I would have no more to do with this unruly group. If they were going to live happily ever after, it was entirely up to them.

# Cast of Characters

| Character Name | Original Position | Transformation |
|---|---|---|
| * Name withheld | A *Good* Fairy | The Same (of course) |
| Estienne the Second | The Prince | The Beast |
| Evan Quillsby | Scribe | The Quill |
| Rebecca Tempera | Artist | The Easel |
| Maximus Stein | Pianist | The Grand Piano |
| Archambault Bellerose | Footman | The Coat Rack |
| Isadora Papier | Library Assistant | The Library Ladder |
| Hugo Livre | Librarian | The Library Painting |
| Theodore Bartleby | Butler | The Armchair |
| Lady Jayne Beatrice Anne Smythe | | |
| | Queen's Secretary | The Bookcase |
| Robert Swisher | Footman | The Mop |
| Charles Melody | Musician | The Cello |
| Victor Viola | Musician | The Violin |
| Darwin Fortier | Guard | The Suit of Armor |
| Frostine Fontaine | Dairy Maid | The Icebox |
| Marthe Tremblay | Scullery Maid | The Mixer |
| Rouge Rubidoux | Parlor Maid | The Dishcloth |

Others who are no longer present:
Queen Marie - Mother of the Prince, passed on years before the curse
Also, King Estienne the First, various Stable Boys, Knights, and the Steward

* At the request of the Good Fairies Guild, the individual name of the Good Fairy has not been included.

## Acknowledgements

Thank you to all of our friends and family for your love and support, and a  special thanks to those who took the time to provide valuable feedback: Robert Gmelin, René Rutter, and Meaghan Morlan.

# About the Authors

**Karen – KD - Blakely (Chapters 7 and 8)** believes life is better when you're owned by a cat, and that you should *never* leave home without a book. Her middle grade/YA fantasy series, The Chimera Chronicles, plunges five friends into a realm of magic and monsters; what begins as an innocent exploration of a strange and fascinating land becomes a dangerous quest. Coming soon, Audrey Murphy, a story of ghosts, greed and redemption — and the first book in the Dark Seighly paranormal romance series, focused around a hidden town that's been guarding a monstrous gateway for nearly 800 years. Find her at www.Kat-Tales.net.

**R. A. Gates (Chapters 5 and 6)** is a single mom of three fantastic kids living in the upper half of California. She loves to read and write urban fantasy because magic is awesome. She's also fairly skilled at binge-watching an entire season on Netflix in one weekend. R. A. has written a short story, The Tenth Life of Mr. Whiskers, and is working on a Pucker Up trilogy in the same world. You can find her on Goodreads, Facebook, and ragates.com. And Panera. She spends the majority of her weekends writing at Panera.

**Kelly Haworth (Chapter 9)** grew up in San Francisco and has been reading science fiction and fantasy classics since she was a kid. She is nonbinary and pansexual and loves to write LGBTQIA characters. She has degrees in both genetics and psychology and works as a project manager at a genetics lab. When not working or writing, Kelly can be found wrangling her two kids, painting, or curled up on the couch with a good TV show or book.

**Jenniffer Lee (Chapters 2 and 4)** is the proud wrangler of three vivacious children, one spunky puppy, and an amazing husband of eleven years. She loves words and children, so she earned a degree to teach with an emphasis in English. She has previously contributed to another anthology, <u>Throbbing Tales: Horror, Humor, Short Stories, and Poetry</u>. Jenniffer is an active member in her local writing community as a co-organizer for her writing group, which was globally recognized by the Meetup.com founders in April 2018.

**Cheryl Mahoney (Chapters 1, 3 and 10)** is the author of the Beyond the Tales quartet, YA fantasy books retelling familiar fairy tales with a twist (and sometimes a talking cat). You may find a certain Good Fairy in the series to be rather familiar! Learn more on Cheryl's blog, Tales of the Marvelous (MarvelousTales.com), where she posts about books and writing. When not telling stories, she also explores amateur drawing, painting and knitting.

You can find them as part of Stonehenge Circle Writers:

| | |
|---|---|
| Twitter: | @StonehengCircle |
| Pinterest: | Stonehenge Circle Writers |
| Facebook: | Stonehenge Circle Writers |
| Goodreads: | Stonehenge Circle Writers |
| Instagram: | Stonehenge_Circle_Writers |
| Blog: | StonehengeCircleWriters.blog |
| Website: | www.StonehengeCircleWriters.com |

## Look for more books by these authors: